# Curious Mem

"Do . . . d'you think, somewhere, there are others like us?"

"Of course."

"Then might I find them one day?"

Magnus took a deep breath and stood as stiff as a stone mouse. "Never say that again! Mice who look like us are kept in cages and come from pet shops. I escaped. You're not going back. A home in a box is no place for a mouse. You belong here with us, with *me*."

Great Uncle Murgatroyd

Mortimer

Madeleine & Maxie

Manuel

Magnus

Miranda

Meggsie

Millie

Mem

Manfred

# Missing Mem

Read both heartwarming adventures by
# ERROL BROOME

---

*Magnus Maybe*

*Missing Mem*

Published by Aladdin Paperbacks

# Missing Mem

ERROL BROOME
Pictures by ANN JAMES

Magnus            Mem

**Aladdin Paperbacks**

New York London Toronto Sydney Singapore

First Aladdin Paperbacks edition February 2003

Originally published in Australia in 2000 by Allen & Unwin
Published by arrangement with Allen & Unwin

ALADDIN PAPERBACKS
An imprint of Simon & Schuster Children's Publishing Division
1230 Avenue of the Americas, New York, NY 10020

Designed by Lisa Vega
The text of this book was set in Simoncini Garamond.

Printed in the United States of America
2 4 6 8 10 9 7 5 3 1

The Library of Congress Control Number 2002101249

ISBN 0-7434-3797-7

# One

The whole world smelled good that day.

Magnus shuffled closer to Miranda and settled into the warm hay, waiting for dusk.

"Comfy, eh?" he whispered.

"Everything's fine," she said.

Yes, he thought, everything was fine. They couldn't have a cozier home than their snuggery, here in the stable loft. The horses below were almost like friends to them.

Then why did his whiskers prickle like this?

His three young ones were beginning to stir, and he could feel Mem's eyes watching him. Something about her troubled him. He stretched his neck and smiled at her—Mem, the only one who'd turned out white like him. She sat apart from her brother and sister as they nudged one another awake.

Manfred wagged his too-long whiskers and nipped Millie's ear.

She squealed and leaped in the air and began to chase him around the loft.

Magnus edged through the hay and huddled beside Mem. "All right there, eh?"

She turned away, and even in the shadows he could see the blush on her ears.

"Come on, you can tell me."

She looked up at him and spoke softly. "Why am I so different?"

"But you're not."

Her eyes were like liquid rubies. She blinked at him. "You know I am."

"You're the same as me. What's wrong with that?"

"Oh, I *want* to be like you."

He touched her gently on her pink nose. "There'll be times, Mem, when it's hard. I know. But here, we're family. You're the same as everyone else."

Manfred and Millie flicked hay in her eyes as they scurried past. Mem snuffled a small sigh. "I miss Madeleine. She was different from other aunts. Why did she have to go?"

"She and Maxie needed to make a home of their own."

"I thought she liked me."

"Everybody likes you," said Magnus.

Mem's voice wavered as if she wasn't sure. "If . . . if I could just find someone like me . . . a friend of my own."

"But Mem, you'll have lots of friends," said Magnus, and in that moment he promised himself that he would always help her. "I *know* you will."

She snuggled against him. "I won't be worworried when you're here."

"*Worried*," he said with a toothy snort. He gazed at his daughter's small, sweet face and the gleaming white of her coat.

"Didn't you notice, Mem, the way Madeleine used to look at you? She'd have given anything to be white, like us."

Her jeweled eyes opened wide. "Truly?"

"Truly. Be proud, Mem, and you'll shine like a star."

Millie was already singing, though it was not yet dark. She and Manfred raced in circles, making tunnels through the hay.

They don't know how lucky they are, thought Magnus. Born in the snuggery, his young had never known the hazards of the house back at *Whereabouts*, where every room hid a trap.

It was there that Magnus had escaped from a cage built to look like a castle. So much had happened since this family of mice had taken him—a strange, white pet mouse—into their home in the linen cupboard. Different though he was, Magnus felt comfortable today among the others, whose coats reflected all the browns and grays of dusty summer paddocks.

"It's boring up here," said Manfred and nipped Millie's tail. "Let's go downstairs and look around."

Magnus stamped his paw on the ground. "Nobody's leaving here till our leader says so. Listen to Mortimer!"

Millie stopped singing and stared at him. "Is anything the matter?"

"Nothing. It isn't time to get up yet. Now go back to sleep."

Magnus had only just closed his eyes again when he felt a warm nose against his cheek.

"There *is* something wrong," whispered Mem. "I can tell by the way you weriggle your nose."

"It's *wiggle*," said Magnus, and gave her ear a lick. "Quiet, Mem. You mustn't worry."

Still, he wished the roan horse would stop coughing. Perhaps that was what he could smell. Germs! Great-uncle Murgatroyd would know. *He* could sniff germs a hedge-length away.

Magnus burrowed through the hay and tapped old Murgatroyd, but he was asleep. Magnus squealed in his ear. Murgatroyd gave a long sputtering snore and didn't open an eye. Let him sleep on, thought Magnus. He'd find out for himself.

He leaned closer to Miranda. "I've got a whiff of something. Did you hear that coughing downstairs? The roan's thrashing around in his stall. We'll have to watch out tonight. I don't want the young ones getting trodden on."

"Mortimer will tell us what to do," said Miranda.

"I'll just slip down anyway, to check on things."

"Be careful." She brushed a paw against his cheek. "We don't want to lose you now."

Magnus grunted. "Do you think I can't look after myself!" He flicked through the hay and scurried down the ladder.

Miranda smiled to herself as she watched him go. How he'd changed from the timid white mouse who'd first come to them!

She hoped he wouldn't ever become too daring.

No sooner had Magnus reached the entrance to the stall than the stable door opened and the farmer came in with another man. The stranger carried a bag.

"Colic," he said when he saw the roan trying to lie down in his stall.

Magnus squatted behind a post while the vet

prodded the roan around the flank and belly. The horse threw up his head and his legs buckled under him. Magnus knew he was in pain. He wanted to cry out to the horse, but he was only an onlooker. He shivered as the vet took out a long needle and gave the roan an injection.

"That might help," said the vet. "But it's serious, I'm afraid."

The farmer wiped his hand across his eyes. "How could it have happened?"

"Moldy hay, perhaps?"

"I don't think so," said the farmer. "But I'll check on it."

"Get him out into the yard, now. Keep him on his

feet. Don't let him get down in his stall."

"I'll get the hand to stay back tonight, then, to keep him walking."

Magnus turned and scampered back upstairs. The drone of snoring came from a corner of the loft. He couldn't believe the family could sleep through all that noise.

But Miranda was awake, and waiting. "Is everything all right?"

"No," whispered Magnus. "The old horse has the colic."

"Will he recover?"

"I hope so. He's my favorite. He's always willing to listen. But one thing I know: There'll be people around here tonight."

This was something they didn't need. Night-time was mouse time, when they were free to roam the stable, pick up spilled grain and steal tidbits left by the farming family.

"We'd better warn Mortimer," said Miranda.

Mortimer was still snoring. These days he and Murgatroyd seldom moved from the snuggery. They sat at the back and chatted about the old days till one of them nodded off.

Magnus nudged Mortimer gently. He shook himself awake and flicked his long, graying whiskers. "Ach! What is it?"

"I need to tell you something."

Mortimer listened. "Is that a fact?" He dragged himself to the centre of the loft and thumped a paw on the wooden floor. "I'll call a meeting. Everybody awake!"

Manuel uncurled from his corner and gazed about. "Wh-what is it?"

"Important," said Magnus. "Just listen."

Mortimer glanced around the group. "Are we all here?" He pointed to himself and then to each one in turn: ". . . six, seven, eight, nine . . . right!"

Meggsie gave a mock bow to show he was listening.

Mortimer waved a paw at him. "You, Meggsie, now you've grown up at last, go and wake Murgatroyd, will you? We may need some of his wisdom tonight."

Meggsie danced across and rubbed Murgatroyd's nose. Then he bent down and bellowed in his ear. Murgatroyd opened one eye. "I hear you."

Mortimer raised his paw. "It's come to my ears that the stable will be busy tonight. The roan is sick with the colic. No one is to go near him, for fear of being trampled. Keep away from big feet. Now we'll leave for the evening feed so we're home before the humans return." He coughed and sank back on his haunches. "And after that, nobody leaves the loft again tonight."

Magnus edged closer to Mortimer. "I think I should tell you one more thing . . . there might be moldy hay."

Miranda gasped. "Not the mold!"

Her ears paled to the color of milk and her eyes misted over. Magnus wished he hadn't felt the need to mention it. Miranda would never forget how their fourth had sickened after finding green cheese. Nothing they had done could revive him. And Marcus, too, long before that. Mold was a curse that would always hang over them.

"Can we c-catch it?" asked Manuel.

"Catch what?" said Murgatroyd.

"The colic."

The old sage blew out his cheeks. "T-t, Manuel, it's a horse disease, not for mice. But we must watch out for moldy hay.' He sighed and sucked on his tongue. "I think I'll stay up here tonight. Meggsie can bring me a seed or two."

Meggsie nodded and turned to his father. "How about you?"

"Ach, since you ask, I'll take a night off too." Mortimer eased back on the hay. "Magnus can take the lead tonight."

"Why me?" asked Magnus.

Mortimer smiled on him. "Magnus, you've come a long way since you first found us."

"Yes, a long way from *Whereabouts*."

"I don't mean distance. I mean you, yourself. Can't you see?"

Magnus peered down his nose, across his chest to his legs. "Not very well."

Mortimer gave a deep squeal of laughter. "Inside

your head, I mean . . . the *whole* mouse!"

"Well, thank you," said Magnus, and hid his head, for he felt that it might burst. Anything he'd learned had come from this gruff mouse in front of him and his Musculus family.

Mortimer sniffed and waved him away. "Ach! Off you go, then."

"Okay," said Magnus. "Meggsie and me. Let's get going, everyone. Scuttle on!"

# Two

The mice scrambled down the ladder, past the chestnut and the bay and the stall where the roan had struggled with his pain.

Magnus and Meggsie led the way across the exercise yard. The farmhand was there, tugging on the roan's bridle, urging him to keep walking.

Beyond the yard, paddocks stretched towards the hills. The yellowing, late-spring grass grew tall, waiting for the slasher to come and cut hay. Already it was beginning to spill its seed. There was plenty for every mouse and still more for next season's greening of the land.

Sunset tilted shafts of orange light through the shadows. Millie sang and skipped across the grass. She and Manfred tripped and tumbled as they nibbled the fresh, nutty seeds. Mem didn't join in their play. She strayed farther till she reached the trees along the fenceline.

Manuel saw her and ran toward the acacia tree.

"Look what I've found," said Mem. "What is it?"

"It's a w-wattle seed. They're special."

"Then I'll save it for later," she said.

Across the grass they heard Magnus call. "What are you two doing over there? Come back!"

"It's all right," said Manuel. "I'm w-watching her." He tapped Mem on the nose. "Come on, then. Don't forget the seed."

The mice grazed together, all except Mem who held so tightly to the wattle seed that her teeth couldn't reach the grass.

Magnus stood and watched as the family foraged. Again tonight, Mem's curiosity had taken her away from the others. Sometimes he worried about where it might lead her. He went over to her. "It's a fine night, yes?"

"Mmm," she said, still clutching the seed.

Meggsie bounced up beside them and winked at Mem. "You'd better watch that one, Magnus. One day she'll wander off and not come back."

Magnus shrugged Meggsie away. "Shh, let me speak with her myself." He edged closer, till his coat brushed against hers. "Now tell me what you're looking for."

"Do . . . d'you think, somewhere, there are others like us?"

"Of course."

"Then might I find them one day?"

Magnus took a deep breath and stood as stiff as a stone mouse. "Never say that again! Mice who look like us are kept in cages and come from pet shops. I escaped. You're not going back. A home in a box is no place for a mouse. You belong here with us, with *me*."

"Yes, yes," she said and clung to the wattle seed as if to show she didn't want to talk any longer.

Night had closed around them. Already they'd been away too long, and Magnus knew he must follow Mortimer's instructions. "Has everybody had enough?" he called. "Time to go, then."

Manuel scurried beside him. "I've c-collected some seed for the old ones."

"Thank you, Manuel. I knew you would."

"I'm supposed to help you," said Meggsie. He jigged up and down on the grass. "I'm pretty good at carting seed."

Magnus smiled. "I remember when you found some in the neighbor's shed. And a lot of good it did us too!" He turned to the other mice. "Straight to the loft, then! No scavenging in the stalls—and no nibbling hay!"

Manfred and Millie streaked ahead, under the stable door and up the ladder to the loft with Mem at their heels. When the others reached the bottom step the three young ones were standing above them, mouths open, waving their paws in the air.

"What's the matter?" called Magnus.

Manfred mouthed the words. "There's a person in the hay."

"A wh-what?" asked Manuel.

"A person!" said Mem in a whisper.

Meggsie chucked Manuel under the snout. "You know, a two-legged one."

"I h-heard. Not in *our* house!"

Magnus pushed the others aside and laid his paws on the bottom rung. "Let me see." He edged his way up the ladder.

It was true! A young man lay stretched in the hay. Magnus sniffed around the sleeping body. "It's the hand."

"What's 'e mean? What's 'e mean?" asked Manfred.

"A hand." Manuel waved up to them. "It's a f-f-f-fact. They call a b-body a hand!"

"A 'hand' is a helper, a farmhand," explained Magnus. "He's supposed to be keeping watch on the roan."

"But he's asleep," said Mem.

The hand breathed like a mountain, heaving out air. Mem craned her neck toward the sleeping form. "Listen! It's like the earth rumblumbling in there!"

"*Rumbling*," said Magnus. "But stand back. Keep out of his way and he won't hurt us." He glanced at Mortimer and Murgatroyd, curled asleep at the back of the loft. "He hasn't disturbed them one bit."

Magnus leaned down and beckoned Miranda, Meggsie, and Manuel to climb the ladder. "Be quiet, lie still, and he'll be gone in the morning."

Meggsie snorted and giggled. "You're not asking us to spend the night with a human!"

"There's room for us all up here."

"But it's not sleep time," said Manfred.

"Shut up and lie still," said Meggsie.

The night lingered on. It seemed the hand would remain in the loft for ever. His stomach rose and fell with the grumble of air from his mouth.

Manfred nudged Millie on her biggest white patch. "D'you think all humans make noises like that?"

"They make lots of different noises," said Mem. "And they smell." She nosed closer and sniffed. "Like old chips, stale and salty." She climbed down the man's leg and nibbled the toe of his boot. "Come and try this, Manny."

Millie's nose quivered, and she held him back. "Mem's silly," she whispered. "Don't go so close."

Mem snuffled as she examined the boot. "I think this thing belongs to a foot. They only have two."

"Because they only have two legs," said Millie.

"Poor things," said Mem. She took a small bite and ran her tongue around her lips. "Nice, but a bit tough, like eating dead cow, I'd say."

Magnus pricked his ears and sat up. "Mem! What do you think you're doing?"

"I'm investertigating," she said.

"*Investigating!*" he said. "And come away from there. *Now!*"

The hand shuddered and sent the three mice scurrying through the hay. Downstairs the walls rattled as the roan kicked at a railing.

Magnus cocked his head and listened. The thrashing below was so loud that it drowned out the sleeping hand's snores.

The roan was in trouble. Magnus couldn't stay there and do nothing. In harder times the roan had so often stood quietly while the mice scrounged grain from the floor of his stall. Never once had he kicked out at them. The roan had helped them to survive. His gentle nicker had welcomed them and told them they were safe in the stable.

The thrashing of hoofs stopped, and Magnus heard only a long, low moan. He'd never heard a horse moan before, and he knew it was a cry for help.

He had to wake the hand. He took a deep breath, crept toward the sleeping man, and bit his ear.

The hand jerked awake. He opened his eyes and sat up.

Magnus buried himself in the hay.

Below, the roan moaned.

The hand shook himself, dusted hay from his shoulders, and almost threw himself down the ladder. He switched on the stable light, took something from his pocket, and pressed buttons that beeped. "Get here, quick!" he yelled.

It seemed like hours, but was perhaps only minutes before the farmer arrived, and then the vet. They spoke softly, as if loud voices might harm the horse.

By now all the mice were awake. Mortimer and Murgatroyd munched on the seeds that Manuel and Meggsie had brought them.

"That was a narrow escape," mumbled Mortimer.

Magnus wondered how Mortimer knew, if he'd been asleep all the time.

"He didn't h-hurt us at all," said Manuel. "That's a f-f-f-fact."

Miranda wagged her head at them and clucked. "He didn't even know we were here. I don't think he has very good whiskers."

"D'you know," interrupted Meggsie. "Some humans don't have any whiskers at all!"

"I'd hate to be human," said Millie. "They've missed out on so many things."

"And they're always pretending." Meggsie pointed a paw to the stable below. "Because they can't see in the dark, they pretend that night is day."

"It's called a light," said Murgatroyd in his long, slow drawl. "Electric light."

Meggsie jigged up and down on the spot to prove how fit he was, but also to show he was bored. "Are they going to stay down there with the roan *all* night? It's such a long time since yesterday."

Yesterday! Where was yesterday? Mem glanced around the loft. "It's a funny thing," she said, and her nose quivered in thought. "Yesterday I found a wattle seed. I still have the seed, but I don't have yesterday. What do you think happens to yesterdays?"

At the back of the snuggery, Murgatroyd lifted

his head and listened and nodded to himself.

Mem watched Magnus and waited for his answer.

"I think yesterday is not any kind of thing," he said. "It's . . . er . . . I mean, you can't hold on to it."

"Then where does it go?" asked Manfred.

Magnus saw that Murgatroyd was awake. "Come!" He beckoned the young towards the old mouse. "We'll ask Murgatroyd."

"Murgatroyd," said Mem. "What happened to yesterday?"

Murgatroyd smiled, as if he liked the question. He took a breath and blew it out through long, crooked teeth. "Yesterday isn't lost." He closed his eyes and coughed. "Ah, it hasn't gone. It's just passed into always."

"See!" said Magnus. "We'll always have it, here, in our heads." He turned back to the old mouse. "Thank you, Murgatroyd. And now, let's have some quiet."

"It's boring, being stuck up here." Millie began to sing again.

"I wish Millie wouldn't sing all the time," said Meggsie. "It irritates me."

"What's 'e mean, *irritate*?" asked Manfred.

"Aggeravate. It aggeravates me too," said Mem.

"*Aggravate!*" said Magnus.

"Ach! Enough of this!" Mortimer shook himself and laid an ear to the floor. "I hear them leaving at last."

The vet's bag snapped shut. "You called just in time. I think we've managed to save him."

"Thank goodness for Ernie," said the farmer. "Good lad, for staying awake!"

"Y-yes," stammered the hand.

"It's almost morning," said the vet. "Get him walking again and see how he goes. With luck, he should be right as rain in a day or two."

"What's 'e mean, what's 'e mean?" asked Manfred.

"That rain is right and no rain is wrong," said Magnus.

Three pairs of feet plodded towards the door. Then the farmer stopped. "What happened to your boots?"

The hand looked down. "Geez! I don't know."

"Tell you what," said the farmer. "For saving the horse's life, I'll buy you a new pair."

I like that! thought Magnus. If it hadn't been for me, the hand would never have woken. But really, I don't suppose *I* could use any boots.

# Three

Dawn slanted through chinks in the stable walls. In the loft the mice were wide awake. Manfred chased Millie along tunnels in the hay. "Come on, Mem," he shouted.

"Can't catch me, can't catch me!" sang Millie, and flipped her tail in Manfred's face.

Mem watched as they raced past, and pretended she didn't want to play. It was time for sleep.

"Got the mulligrubs again?" called Manfred.

"Haven't," said Mem, and buried her pink nose in the hay. She knew that Magnus was irritated by these silly games. More than anything, she wanted to please her father. She wanted to be like him. How could she grow up like Magnus and be like the others too?

Manfred and Millie giggled and rolled about. Millie pinched his whiskers, which were already as long as Mortimer's. Manfred nipped her on her middle-sized white patch.

Mem studied Millie's mottled coat. It was a bit like the roan's, all muddled up. Yet Millie didn't care what she looked like. She was only muddled on the outside.

Mem waited with her eyes shut and listened to the giggles and squeals till Mortimer called, "Quiet! Time for sleep."

When the loft had settled into silence, Magnus whispered to Miranda. "Something's going to happen. I can feel it. I think I'll go and have a sniff around downstairs."

He made his way to the roan's stall. The horse was there again, lying quietly now with his head on the hay. Magnus stopped beside him and gazed at the sleeping animal. He nibbled spilled grain on the floor.

The roan opened an eye and looked at him. Magnus didn't know how to tell him, "I'm glad you're alive." He stood, watching the horse till the stable door jolted open.

Magnus scurried behind a post.

The farmer and the hand came into the stall. The farmer ran his fingers over the roan's flank and patted his head. "You're okay there." He turned to the hand.

"He'll be fine again soon, but it was a close call. We can't take any risks, so first thing is to get rid of that hay."

The hand picked up a huge pitchfork and climbed the ladder to the loft. He swung the fork into the hay, spiking a bale on the long prongs.

Magnus burst from his hiding place and dashed toward the ladder. "No! No! They'll all be killed!"

The hand took no notice. He tossed bale after bale to the ground.

The farmer trudged from the stall as Magnus flashed past him. "There's a ruddy mouse!" He picked up the stable broom and thwacked it into the ground just a crumb away from where Magnus stood.

Magnus bolted through a slit in the floor.

The farmer carted out the first hay bales and began

to load his trailer. Magnus pushed his nose between the floorboards. The hand was still pitching his fork into the hay.

"Help! Stop!" shouted Magnus. "Miranda's in there! Our young are in there! Manuel! Meggsie! All of them! Help!"

The hand stabbed his fork into the very center of the loft. The mice squealed and leaped in the air. They jumped and flew, head first, upside down, somersaulting like firecrackers that had just been set alight.

Magnus watched from below and held his breath. He shut his eyes. Surely they would all be spiked to death.

"Jeez, oh, jeez!" shouted the hand. "They're everywhere!"

"Keep going," said the farmer. "I'll fix 'em later. I've been promising my girl a cat for ages."

The mice cried out and fled to every corner of the loft where a crack or crevice might hide them.

The hand raised his fork to scoop up the last bale. He didn't see an old graying mouse with long whiskers crouched in a corner behind the hay.

When he lunged with the fork, he heard the squeal. He held the fork high and shook the small shape to the boards. "Jeez, oh jeez, I got one!" Then he turned and tramped down the ladder.

Magnus waited till the truck drove away before he dragged himself up the rungs. He took slow, deep breaths and slow, short steps, afraid of what he might discover when he reached the top.

At first he thought the loft was empty. But then, in a corner, he saw the bloodied body.

"Mortimer!" He rushed to his side, and laid his head on Mortimer's neck. "Say something." There was

no reply. No sound,
no breath.

Magnus looked
around, searching for
someone to speak to, yet he
couldn't speak. He opened his mouth and no sound
came. This was the mouse, Mortimer, who taught him
to be a mouse. Mortimer had accepted him, and so
led the others to believe in him too.

Mortimer was old and didn't have much more
time. It wasn't right that he should go this way.

Magnus stood beside him, shaking his head, staring at the walls and seeing nothing. He didn't hear the
rustle of other mice squeezing back through the cracks.

They gathered around the body, and nobody
spoke. Then Murgatroyd pushed into the center of
their circle. He cleared his throat. "Mortimer won't
want us to be miserable. He led us well. There was little
more for him to give. He was happy." He raised his
head and gazed around the group. "I only ask you to
remember all he has taught us."

The mice stood in silence, and of those who had
cuts and bumps and bruises, not one felt their own
pain.

"As soon as it's dark," said Murgatroyd, "we'll take him back to the hills."

"And then what will we do?" asked Meggsie.

They all felt at a loss.

"We think before we do anything," said Murgatroyd. "For a while we'll have to lie low, but we don't move from our snuggery."

By moonshine they carried Mortimer across the paddock.

Murgatroyd shuffled at the head, with the strong ones bearing the body. Meggsie limped. An old wound had been reopened, but he hardly noticed it. Dried blood caked Manuel's thigh, and Mem's white coat was smeared and tatty.

When they reached the trees, they stopped to rest.

Suddenly Manfred gasped. "Mem! Look at your tail! What happened?"

Mem curled her tail quickly under her body. Her pale ears turned pink. "I'm all right. It's nothing."

"But . . . but . . ."

"It's cut off!" cried Millie.

Mem shuffled where she sat. "It isn't. Just a bit, then. The fork hit me before I got away. It hurt . . . but I can't feel it now."

"Let me see," said Magnus. It had to be Mem, he thought. Had she stayed too long in the snuggery, to see what was going on? Or to help Mortimer perhaps? She'd never say.

He clicked his teeth when he saw the wound. "Good gruntle, Mem! Why didn't you tell us? It needs a decent lick and clean."

"I *have* licked it," she said. "I wish you'd stop staring. It's *all right*."

Miranda puckered her nose at the others. "Leave her alone now. Can't you understand?" she croaked to Manfred. "Mem doesn't want us to see. Nobody likes to lose the tip of their tail."

"Poor Mem," muttered Magnus. "It's bad enough

being white. Now this." He nudged her with his nose and gently licked the raw end of her tail. "There, Mem, it's healing already." He saw the quiver in her eyes. "Why, no other mouse will ever notice."

He nodded to Manfred and Millie and spoke through his teeth. "Don't you ever dare tease her about this!"

Mem uncurled, and the mice pushed on in silence, carrying their load.

They laid Mortimer under the roots of a gnarled stringybark.

"It's time to leave him now," said Murgatroyd.

They stood, not wanting to move, not able to say good-bye.

Millie edged towards Magnus and slipped her paw into his.

"I don't know what to say," she whimpered.

"Then sing for him," he said.

Millie gazed into the night that enfolded them, and it seemed the words of her song had always been inside her.

The mice bowed their heads as she sang, and when she came to the end, they looked at one another in silence.

"Our grandfather," said Mem.

"Our f-father," said Manuel.

Murgatroyd stepped into the circle and raised his paw. "Come, now. We've said good-bye." He turned to Mem and nudged her on the snout. "Smile now," he said, and led them away.

# Four

The mice stared at one another across the bare boards.

Their loft was cold and uncomforting, with nowhere to hide. Red blotches still smudged the floorboards. But soon the farmer would buy in more hay. Sweet, fresh hay, as good for mice as it would be for horses.

Murgatroyd coughed from the back of the loft. Where the two old mice had squatted together Murgatroyd now sat alone. He beckoned to Magnus. "Good fellow, it's time we had another talk."

Magnus wondered how long Murgatroyd would stay awake. His eyes kept closing as he spoke. But even a few words from Murgatroyd were worth hearing.

Magnus waited.

Murgatroyd shuffled on his haunches and raised his head from his chest. "Mortimer was pleased with you."

"Thank you."

"He . . . er . . ." His voice trailed away.

"Yes?" said Magnus.

"Yes." Murgatroyd shook himself. "We have no leader now."

"We'll manage," said Magnus. "You and Mortimer have taught us how."

"No, no." Murgatroyd's paw wavered through the air. "*You* will manage. You must be the leader. It's what Mortimer wanted."

"Me?" Magnus gulped. "Why me?"

"Must you always say that, my good fellow? There's no need for such modesty. It's time you learned to know yourself."

"Well, thank you," said Magnus. It was all he could think to say.

Murgatroyd beckoned him closer. "Have you noticed if you stand back from the hills you can see more?"

Magnus nodded.

"Then stand back from yourself, my good fellow, and you will understand more."

Magnus couldn't remember leaving Murgatroyd or walking back to join Miranda. His heart thumped like a bat's wings, and everything else had blown from his head.

"Mortimer chose me to be leader!" he blurted to Miranda. "Can you believe it?"

She wiped her paw gently across his snout. "Of course. I always knew it."

Magnus didn't want to be bossy. He edged around the loft, telling each mouse in turn that it was time for the evening forage.

Meggsie slapped him on the back of the neck. "Okay, boss! Lead the way!"

"We'll do it together, you and me," said Magnus.

Meggsie stood back and stared at Magnus. "Don't you *ever* learn! *You're* the one, not me—and I don't want to be. I want to have fun. I want to be the favorite uncle. I'm not the serious type."

Magnus wiggled his nose and nodded. "I suppose I *am* fairly serious about most things."

"That's right for you," said Meggsie. "Don't get

me wrong; stay the way you are and let me be myself too, okay? Since you joined our family, things have been a whole lot better for me."

Magnus gulped. Every day, he was learning something new. He brushed the dust from his whiskers and led the mice down the ladder.

The farmer came early next morning to check on the roan and to lead the chestnut and the bay into the exercise yard.

The hand mucked out the stalls and filled the water troughs. "What've you done about the mice?"

"Wait till you see what's arriving this afternoon," said the farmer.

From their not-so-snuggery in the loft, Magnus and the Musculus family listened.

"What could it be?" asked Miranda.

"A new pony?" said Mem.

"A canary?" said Millie.

"A great fat pumpkin?" said Manfred.

Something to worry about, thought Magnus, because he knew. But he bit back his words. "Let's wait and see."

They didn't have long to wait, for while they were dozing in the afternoon, the woman and the girl came to saddle up the horses.

The girl carried something in her arms.

"It's a c-cat!" said Manuel.

Magnus peered down from the loft. "It's only a baby." But it would grow into a cat—and soon. "We'll need to find a way to beat it. I'll have to ask Murgatroyd."

Murgatroyd waved him away. "It's up to you now." He closed his eyes. "You'll work it out."

What do they think I am? thought Magnus. They're making me do everything.

Meggsie growled beside him. "If the cat stays, I go!"

"Calm down, Meggsie," said Magnus. "I'll think of something."

The woman tightened the chestnut's girth and told the girl to saddle up the bay.

"What will I do with the kitten?" asked the girl.

The woman pointed to a blanket in the feed room. "Put her down there and shut the door. She'll be right."

The kitten's locked in for now, thought Magnus. It gave him time to think. He watched the woman and the girl ride away. "I want everyone to stay up here," he said. "But I'm going down. I've decided to make friends with this kitten."

"Friends!" shouted Meggsie. "You must be mad!"

"Friends are better than enemies," said Magnus.

"But I don't like your chances."

"It's worth a try."

Miranda dragged him back by the tail. "Listen to me a minute! That animal might only be a kitten, but it's already a giant beside all of us. Please, Magnus, be careful."

"You're always telling me to be careful."

"We don't want you to go," said Millie.

"Kittens bite," said Manfred.

"Don't be ferightened," said Mem.

"*Frightened!*" said Magnus. "And I'm not. Now, will you please let me go!"

# Five

**M**agnus squeezed under the door into the feed room. The whole space was no bigger than a cupboard, with a chair jammed into one corner and grain bins stacked side by side. Each one had a tight-fitting lid.

An old horse rug lay inside the door. The kitten merged into the graying blanket, so that for a moment Magnus didn't see her. But he could smell cat.

The kitten smelled mouse. She uncurled, pulled herself up on stiff legs, and glared at him. Her back arched like a hairpin.

It wasn't a very good start.

The kitten loomed over Magnus, as big as a pademelon.

"Hi there," he squeaked.

The kitten hissed.

"Welcome to the stable."

The kitten focused her eyes on Magnus. She straightened her back and dug her front paws into the blanket. All the time, she stared at him.

"Are you staying here?" he asked.

The kitten clawed the blanket.

"We live here too." He wished she would answer him. "Can't we be friends?"

The kitten didn't seem to think so. She stretched her neck and looked ready to pounce.

Magnus held his breath. Don't be afraid, he told himself. You're older than she is. "I wonder what you might like to eat," he said, and knew straight away it was a silly question. He didn't want to hear the answer. "I . . . we could find nice things . . . have a party, perhaps."

The kitten didn't understand. She lifted her head and sat back on the blanket.

Magnus gazed around, wondering what to try next. Under the door, he saw a thread of whisker and the tip of a small pink nose.

"Mem! What are you doing here?"

She pushed her head into the feed room. "I'm . . .
I was wondering . . ."

"Go back up! This minute!"

Mem jerked back and disappeared.

Magnus blew out his cheeks and muttered, "What
will that mouse do next!" He shook himself and turned
back to the kitten to find her face right next to his.

"Oh! Wh-where were we now?" he said in a shaky
voice. "Oh, yes. I wanted to show you something."

He jigged nervously on one leg and then the other,
faster and faster. "Look, I can run in circles! I can
chase my tail!" He stepped out of a spin and eyed the
kitten dizzily. "I bet you can't do that!"

The kitten wrapped her tail around her body and
watched him without a flicker of movement. Her eyes
were the color of new spring leaves.

Magnus waved his paws in the air and swayed in a circle. "Bet you can't!" he chanted.

He paused for a moment to catch his breath, then away he whirled again. "Have a try! Go on, have a try!"

With one swipe, the kitten cuffed him and sent him reeling.

Magnus jolted to a standstill and glared at the kitten, but she sank her head on her paws and closed her eyes.

"Well, all right, if that's what you think." She isn't very friendly, he thought. But at least she didn't bite me.

Meggsie peered down as Magnus climbed the ladder to the loft. "What've you been doing?"

"Talking to the kitten."

"You've . . . WHAT?"

"I've been talking to the kitten, but she didn't seem to want to talk to me."

"You're off your head," said Meggsie. "Don't ask *me* to talk to a cat."

"Oh, I never would. I'll do it myself." He glanced around the loft till he saw Mem. "Come here!" he called. "What do you think you were doing down there?"

The blush flooded back to her ears. "I thought
. . . I was thinking the kitten might be lonely."

"The kitten is *my* business, Mem. Leave it to me."
He leaned closer to her. "But if you really want to
know, I'm getting to know the kitten. A cat could be a
useful friend."

She twitched her nose and gave him a puzzled
look. "You mean . . . not like a *real* friend?"

Magnus clicked his teeth at her. Mem would never
understand.

They heard hoofs cantering in the distance and a
clang of gates. The woman and the girl led their horses
into the stable, brushed them down and fed them,
then went to talk to the roan.

When they left, the girl had the kitten in her arms.

Magnus watched them go, but the kitten didn't
sneak even a look towards the loft.

He shrugged. "That's that for today, then! I'll have
another go tomorrow."

The farmer's tractor chugged toward the stable
early next morning while the mice huddled together
to keep warm. The crisp air stung their skin, and

they longed for fresh hay to blanket them.

"It's ages since we've had a good day's sleep," said Magnus.

Murgatroyd stirred himself. "But we haven't long to wait. Listen!"

Meggsie stared at the old mouse. "Can you hear that? I thought you were deaf."

"I hear what I need to hear, young chap." He hauled himself to his feet. "And now, I think we should all clear out of this place."

Magnus nodded across to him and gave the order. "Everybody out!"

Murgatroyd hobbled after the mice as they scattered through chinks in the wall. Downstairs the hand mucked out the stalls. The farmer carted hay to the foot of the ladder and pitched bales into the loft. Thud after thud rocked the mice as they clung to a narrow plinth on the outer wall.

At last there was calm. The men's voices faded away, and the tractor started up again.

"There," said Magnus as he led the mice back to their snuggery. "Better than ever!"

"I didn't ever w-worry," said Manuel. "You told us the hay would come."

"Yes," said Magnus. "I knew."

"Bit of a smart aleck, aren't you?" said Meggsie.

"What's 'e mean, what's 'e mean?" asked Manfred.

"He means berainy," said Mem.

"*Brainy!*" shouted Magnus. "Good gruntle, Mem, can't you get anything right!"

Miranda rushed at him and pulled him aside. "Leave her alone!" she rasped. "You're always correcting her."

"Can't she learn to speak properly, like the rest of us!"

"I seem to remember you didn't always get the words right yourself."

Magnus breathed a long, slow sigh. "I suppose I get a bit irritated at times."

"It isn't because she's white, is it?"

He jerked his head towards her. "And what do you mean by *that*?"

"It's just . . . that you seem to pick on her a lot. You should love her all the more because she's white, like you."

"Please don't remind me, Miranda. Lately, I've been able to forget that I'm white."

She stared him straight in the eye. "And I liked you more when you remembered."

Her words stung him like a scorpion. For a moment he couldn't move. Then he crept to her and nuzzled her chin. "Thank you for telling me."

# Six

Magnus wondered if he had some sort of clock inside his head. The click of the stable door woke him like an alarm. He pricked his ears and listened.

The woman and the girl were there again, and the kitten.

He settled back, waiting till they locked the kitten in the feed room. Around him, the mice snuggled like fluffy balls in the warm hay. Nobody stirred, even to the sounds of Millie singing in her sleep.

Without waking anyone, Magnus scrambled down the ladder to the stables. The roan horse twitched his tail and neighed when Magnus climbed on the feed trough.

"I'm pleased you're well again," said Magnus.

The horse nickered softly.

"I need to ask your advice."

The roan stretched his neck till Magnus could feel the steam from his nostrils. He made himself more

comfortable on the rim of the trough. "You see, we have all these problems. First we lost Mortimer when they cleared out the hay. Now the girl has a kitten. Our lives won't be worth living with a cat in the stable."

He waved a paw to make sure the roan was listening. "So what do you think we should do?"

The roan chomped on the hay and tossed his head.

"I was thinking, if we could make friends with the cat . . ."

The roan laid back his ears. Magnus waited, but the horse made no sound.

"You're not much help," muttered Magnus, and

stole a mouthful of bran mash before he left the stall.

The kitten lay curled on the blanket inside the feed room.

"It's me again!" said Magnus as he pushed under the door.

The kitten lifted her head.

"I'm sorry I couldn't find anything to bring you."

The kitten watched closely. Her green eyes were like mirrors, where Magnus saw himself so small and so white.

"How are you getting on?"

The kitten didn't move.

"I mean, do they treat you well?"

Why do these other animals leave all the talking to me? thought Magnus. "Haven't you got anything to say?"

He decided to try something different. He darted forward and nipped the kitten's leg.

The kitten smacked out her paw as if she were tapping at a fly.

So! thought Magnus, and he determined to be brave. "Bite me! I dare you!" he cried.

The kitten took no notice.

"Come on, let's have a game. Let's play dares."

She isn't interested, he thought. Or else she thinks I'm a fool. Well, good riddance! He flounced away, and disappeared under the door.

But he wouldn't give up. Every afternoon, Magnus put his plan into action. He talked to the kitten and tried everything he could think of to turn her into a friend.

He began to feel he was only an annoyance. And he felt weary. While the other mice slept in the snuggery, he was downstairs using up all his energy and brains on a kitten.

On the fifth day, the door to the feed room was open. The girl trusted the kitten now not to run away.

"I brought you something," said Magnus. "The girl must have dropped it." He pushed a scrap of peanut-butter sandwich across the floor.

The kitten nudged the crust with her nose and gulped it down.

"Did you like it?"

The kitten swallowed again and sat back on her haunches.

"Tomorrow I'll find you something special."

So on the sixth day, Magnus left the snuggery earlier in the afternoon and ran down to the creek. He sat on the bank and peered into the shallow water, but could see nothing that would do for a kitten. Nor were there any scraps on the path.

He'd almost given up when he saw a feather flickering in the breeze. He scurried across the plowed paddock. There, half hidden in a furrow, lay a dead sparrow. Magnus could see where the tractor's tracks had run right over it.

The bird was bigger than Magnus himself. He grasped it between his teeth and began to drag it to the stable. His mouth was full of feathers. He could hardly breathe. Many times he stopped for breath and to rest his legs.

When he reached the stable, he burst into the feed room. "There! Look what I've brought today!"

The kitten nosed the bird and flicked it with her paw. The wing feathers fluttered as if the sparrow were still alive.

"Murgatroyd once told me that cats like fish," said Magnus. "I tried to get you a tadpole, but then I found this bird."

The kitten tapped the sparrow with one paw and then the other and picked it up in her mouth.

Magnus laughed. "You look as if you have a great brown beard!" He stopped and stepped back. "Oh, sorry, sorry. I didn't mean it."

The kitten dropped the bird and tugged at it with her paws. She stripped away feathers with her teeth and sat down to gnaw the flesh.

"I'll be off, then," said Magnus. "See you tomorrow."

But on the seventh day, he stayed in the loft. He was tired, worn out with all this effort. He wouldn't visit the kitten that afternoon. He'd find out whether she missed him. Ah, it was good to have a day off!

Mem raised her head and sniffed about her. Except for Murgatroyd's wheezing snores, the snuggery was silent. Even Magnus was asleep.

She slipped down the ladder to the feed room. The kitten was not there, so she scuttled across the stable floor and into the yard.

She'd never been alone in the open before. And in

daylight. The air was heavy with the muggy smell of grass. Around her, paddocks reached out to the sky-line. Suddenly she wasn't sure why she'd come or what she was looking for.

She twitched her whiskers and thought it might be a good idea to go back inside. As she turned, she saw the kitten creeping from behind the stable.

It was too late to run. Perhaps, if she stood quite still, the kitten might not notice her. After all, I *am* rather small, she thought.

The kitten stopped for a moment and mewed.

"Hello," said Mem in a voice she could hardly hear herself.

The kitten sat and stared at her with big green eyes.

"I've been thinking about you," said Mem. "About how brave you must be. You don't seem to have any family. Are you really all alone?"

The kitten stood up and took another slow step towards Mem.

"Were you taken away from your mother to be brought here?"

Mem waited for the kitten to say something. Perhaps she didn't want to talk. "It's all right," she said. "You don't have to tell me if you don't want to."

The kitten lifted a front paw and trod down warily. She took a halting step and miaowed.

"Oh!" cried Mem. "What's wrong?"

The kitten eased back on her haunches and licked a front paw.

"Are you all right?"

The kitten stood on three legs and limped closer to where Mem stood.

I wish I could stop shaking, thought Mem. She nosed across the grass towards the kitten. "Can't you tell me what happened?"

The kitten hung her head.

"You *do* look miserable. Let me help." Mem edged closer till she could feel the kitten's breath on her face. "Can't you take one more step?"

The kitten lay on her side with her paws stretched in front of her.

Mem crept between the furry legs and sniffed at the leather-patch feet. A needle-like claw scraped her cheek. "Ouch!" she cried, and jerked away.

The kitten shuddered.

"It's all right," said Mem. "I know you didn't mean it." She peered at the pad on the right front paw. "Now look, I can see blood. It's red. You must have cut yourself." She buried her nose into the foot. "And there's something else. It's a prickle—gone right in. You'll never get it out."

The kitten miaowed.

"But *I* can."

Mem tugged on the prickle with her long, sharp top teeth. The point snapped off in her mouth, and she swallowed it. It tasted like any other dried seed. She'd have to dig in deeper.

"This might hurt a bit. I'll try gnawing it out."

The kitten made no sound.

"I *knew* you were brave," said Mem. "If you just lie still, I'll get in there."

"Miaow!" The kitten pulled back.

"I know, I know. Sorry. Just a moment and I'll have it." Mem burrowed in again and nibbled a little bit more, and more, till only the tiniest splinter remained in the flesh. She seized it between her tweezer-teeth and slowly-slowly squeezed it from the paw.

Mem spat out the scrap of prickle. "See? It's all gone!"

The kitten lifted her paw and licked the wound. Again and again, she rubbed her tongue over the sore patch, till there was no blood left. Then she pulled herself to her feet and placed the injured paw on the ground. She took a step, and another, and skipped across the yard.

Mem laughed at the kitten's antics. "Hey!" she yelled and rolled about on the grass. But she reminded herself, *this is a cat*. "I think I might hurry a bit," she said, and scurried home to the loft.

Back in the snuggery, Mem fell into a deep sleep. Magnus was dozing when he felt vibrations on the ladder. He nudged Miranda. "Someone's coming!"

Miranda jolted awake. Her whiskers bristled. "Quick! Tell them all to run!"

Magnus opened his mouth to speak, but it was too late. He found himself face to face with the kitten.

She miaowed. One by one, the mice leaped to their feet. They stood as if glued to the hay. he kitten watched them. Her mouth curled into a half-moon shape.

"It'll eat us all!" cried Manuel.

"Leave this to me!" Magnus pushed himself between the kitten and his family. "What is it you want?"

She gazed around the loft, from mouse to mouse, as if she were counting them. A soft drone like an engine came from her throat.

The mice stood, too terrified to move. All except Mem, who was still not fully awake. She uncurled and watched with sleepy, uncertain eyes as the kitten groped forward and sniffed the hay. With high, slow steps, she tiptoed across the snuggery towards Mem.

"What's she doing? Where's she going?" whispered Manfred.

"Shh," said Miranda. "Don't move."

They held their breath as the kitten moved in slow motion, her eyes fixed on the spot where Mem lay. She

stopped for a moment, bent down, and rubbed her
nose gently against Mem's.

Then she turned slowly and walked towards the
ladder.

Magnus stood by the top rung and nodded to the
kitten. "Nice to see you again."

The kitten flung out her paw and pinned his tail
to the boards.

The mice gasped. But, as quickly as she'd lashed
out, the kitten pulled back her paw and set her feet
on the ladder.

Magnus caught his breath and steadied himself
against Miranda. "Just a bit of fun," he said with something like a grin.

The mice gazed at him and at one another. For a few minutes they'd shared their snuggery with a cat! Life would never be the same again.

"How did you do it?" they asked.

Magnus puffed out his chest. "It was nothing." Yet he had to admit that, right now, he felt pretty pleased with himself.

"Tell us, tell us," said Manuel.

Mem stayed silent, and Magnus didn't look in her direction. He nodded to the old mouse in the corner. "Murgatroyd has taught me to think." He'd listened and he'd learned. And now, if he could make friends with a cat, who else might become his friend? He could mix with important animals—humans, even. After all, hadn't he once known a boy? Before he met the Musculus family, hadn't he lived in a kind of castle?

He stretched out in the hay and looked at himself, close up, and he liked what he saw. Maybe he was still a small mouse, but inside himself he felt big.

# Seven

Just before dawn they heard the clatter and hum of trucks along the highway. In the distance, headlights flashed between the trees.

"It's a pro-procession," said Manuel.

"Hmph!" Murgatroyd coughed. "The circus is back."

"What's a circus?" asked Manfred.

"A show on wheels," said Manuel. "And that's a f-f-f-fact."

Murgatroyd opened one eye. ". . . a show where animals pretend to be people," he said in a creaky voice. "And people pretend to be birds."

"What's 'e mean?" asked Manfred.

"Well," said Magnus. "I think they fly."

"Sounds like fun," said Meggsie. "And I wouldn't mind a bit of fun right now."

"Me too," squeaked Mem.

She crept up to Magnus and prodded him with her nose. "Are you listening?"

He turned to her slowly.

Her small, bright eyes smiled up at him. "Can we go somewhere fun?"

He rubbed his whiskers against her cheek and spoke gently. "Not today, Mem."

"Why not!" shouted Millie.

"You used to take us places," said Manfred. "And show us things."

"I wasn't so busy then."

Meggsie jumped up and flashed his toothy grin. "I'll take you. How about the circus?"

Magnus shook his head. "The circus is no place for a mouse. I've heard there are animals as tall as buildings and humans with big feet and machines that whisk you around in circles." Besides, he had better things to do. He had a brain, hadn't he proved it? And he wasn't going to stop using it now.

"I'll look after them," said Meggsie. "So who's coming?" He nodded his head to each one in turn: "Manuel, Manfred, Millie, and Mem, okay. Anyone else?"

Murgatroyd shuffled his legs and began to cough. His body shook like a bag of bones. Day by day he was growing thinner. He looked at Meggsie through watery eyes and tried to speak.

"What's that, Murgatroyd?" said Meggsie.

Murgatroyd wheezed and drooped his head on his chest. In an instant Miranda was beside him. "I'll stay with Murgatroyd. He needs me. But you'll go, won't you, Magnus?"

"No." His answer was quick. "Meggsie can manage." He tried not to notice the uneasy feeling in his stomach. Something told him he should go with them, keep an eye on them. But he pushed away his doubts. They'd be all right. And he had too much else to think about. Yes, Meggsie could manage.

"Tomorrow, then," said Meggsie. "The five of us."

In the lull of afternoon, Magnus breathed a long, slow sigh. It was peaceful in the snuggery with just Miranda and Murgatroyd. The others had been gone since early morning. He winked at Miranda. "At last we have time to think. And I might have another word with Murgatroyd."

He sat down beside the old sage and said, "Excuse me . . ."

Murgatroyd opened an eye. "My good fellow, I have told you . . . everything . . . I know."

Magnus could see the old mouse was fading away. He drew closer and put his ear against Murgatroyd's mouth.

"It's up to you now, Magnus. You have the brains to see . . . which way . . . you're going."

The effort of talking had drained all his strength. Murgatroyd's jaw trembled, and he began to gasp. Magnus reached out his paw and touched him gently on the shoulder. "Murgatroyd, thank you."

Miranda was watching with darkness in her eyes. She drew closer to Murgatroyd and rubbed her nose against his cheek.

Magnus knew Murgatroyd would give no more advice. To anyone. He and Miranda sat with him as his breaths grew noisier and slower, till each one seemed to be his last.

Then the old mouse shuffled to his feet.

"Stay, Murgatroyd," said Miranda. "We're here."

Murgatroyd held up a shaky paw and staggered towards the ladder.

"No! You'll fall!" cried Magnus.

Murgatroyd turned and gazed into Magnus's eyes.

"I . . . am . . . leaving. Let me go." His words were a string of bubbles, dissolving in the air.

Magnus stood aside, holding his breath as Murgatroyd stumbled down the ladder. Without looking back, the old mouse hobbled across the stable into the yard.

"Aren't we going to stop him?" Magnus asked.

Miranda shook her head. "Let him go."

They waited till Murgatroyd was out of sight, then they crept down the ladder and into the sunlight. Magnus slipped his paw into Miranda's, and together they stood and watched Murgatroyd limp across the paddock. Slowly, painfully slowly, the figure grew smaller until it was lost in the landscape.

"Good night, Murgatroyd," whispered Magnus, though it was still bright, white day.

Murgatroyd had gone to the hills he knew, the hills that made even humans look small.

Miranda sneaked away and curled back in the loft, alone.

Magnus wasn't aware of time. For a moment or an hour he stood in the yard, while all the things Murgatroyd had taught him passed through his head. His mind drifted apart till he saw himself from a distance, and Murgatroyd's words became clear to him.

"It's up to me now," he said. So many thoughts, so many ideas crowded into his mind that he felt his head might burst.

He decided he'd have another talk to the roan.

The horse stood placidly in his stall. He flicked his tail when Magnus climbed on the feed trough.

"Hi," said Magnus.

The roan nosed the edge of the trough.

"I need to speak with you again. Suddenly things have changed. Old Murgatroyd's gone. I'm in the front line now. In other words, I'm in charge."

The roan twitched his nostrils.

"Now they all depend on me. I want to do what's best for all of us. And I want them to look up to me." He tapped his paw on the trough and gazed up at the roan's deepwater eyes. "Is that right, do you think?"

The roan stared back at him and munched on the hay.

"You see," continued Magnus, "I started off as a nobody, and I've learned a lot, so . . ." Out of the corner of his eye, he saw a flash of color. A page torn from a weekly magazine lay on the floor at the back of the stall. The bright gloss lured him down to look.

"What's this? A house? Do people really live in such places?"

FOR SALE said a sign across the bottom.

Magnus had never seen a grander house. It had more doors than the stable had mouseholes and more windows than chinks in the snuggery walls. When summer came the flowers in the garden would shed a million seeds. Surely it was some sort of palace, a castle even. Hadn't Madeleine believed he'd grown up in a castle? Because of his handsome white coat and polite manner, he'd always appeared special to her.

He wondered whether she and Maxie had found a place like this? Surely not! *I* deserve better than they do, he thought. I'm friend to kitten and horse. *I'm* the one who should be living in this house.

He looked up at the roan. "It could suit us rather well, don't you think? I don't mean to be rude, but living in a stable isn't all that grand."

Magnus tapped a paw on the picture of the house. "You don't happen to know where this place is?"

The roan kept on munching.

"I don't suppose you can read, either. But look, I know those trees. I'll find it!" He knew he would.

The roan flicked his tail across his rump.

"Thanks a lot," said Magnus. Now I must be off." He had no time to waste. Without going upstairs to say good-bye to Miranda, he sped into the yard. Everything else was forgotten, for he was about to find something special, a bit like a castle perhaps.

# Eight

Meggsie and Manuel and the three young mice set out early for the circus. A quick scamper across the paddocks took them to the gravel road leading to the river. Over the bridge the road twisted toward town.

Meggsie stopped to rest behind a bus shelter. He cocked his head and pricked his whiskers. "Listen! You can hear the sounds of the circus."

"It isn't sc-scary, is it?" asked Manuel.

"Only a bit," said Meggsie, though he wasn't sure what to expect around the next bend in the road.

Manuel ran across to Mem and patted her on the nose. "Don't worry, Mem. I'll look after you."

Mem shook him away. "I'm not worworried." Why should she be afraid of circuses? "I'm not a baby, you know."

The town reserve had become a city of caravans and wagons. A giant striped tent rose above the roofs, with a trail of people twining like a caterpillar around the entrance.

"That must be the Big Top," said Meggsie.

Outside, a merry-go-round whirled and played.

"Horses!" cried Manfred. "But they have no smell—except paint."

"Because they aren't real," said Meggsie. "Come on, I'll take you for a ride."

"Dollar a spin!" called a man with a bag of money around his waist.

"Don't listen to him," said Meggsie. "Just slip on here."

One by one, they scrambled up the step to the merry-go-round. It was a steep climb for a mouse, and some small humans needed a lift to the platform.

Meggsie led them to a stocky wooden horse with a big black saddle. "Climb up here," he said, pointing to a hoof that rested just above the floor.

The mice clambered up the leg to the rump and on to the saddle. "Whee! Look down there!" sang Millie.

"Stick together," warned Meggsie. "And don't fall off."

"Wh-what if we're seen?" asked Manuel.

"We won't be. Everyone's looking at someone they know—and they don't know us!"

"Hold on! Hold on!" sang Millie as music blared and the horse began to glide up and down. The floor was moving beneath them. Children waved and cried out, "Look at me!"

"See," whispered Meggsie. "Nobody's looking at us."

"Where are we going then?" asked Manfred.

"Up and down and round and round," said Meggsie. "Stay where you are."

My head's going round in circles too, thought Mem, as they whirled past the spot where they started.

"Are you all r-r-right?" asked Manuel.

She wobbled her nose and nodded.

"You're very white."

"Of course I am!" Was this all there was to a merry-go-round? The horses back at the stable smelled much better, and they didn't go around in circles.

At last she felt the world slowing down, and the music faded as the merry-go-round wound to a stop. Mem's head still spun. She stepped to the edge of the platform and toppled to the ground.

"This afternoon's performance is about to begin," announced a very loud voice.

She picked herself up, and a tremor of excitement ran through her body. Behind her she heard the thump of feet and murmur of voices. A dog barked close by. Mem turned to find a jumble of animals assembled about her.

They couldn't see her squatting under the rope beside a tent peg. Four white ponies with gilded horns on their heads pranced on the spot, eager to enter the ring. A black poodle balanced on each pony's back.

Mem dug herself into the dirt behind the tent peg and watched.

"Hurry up, Mem!" called Meggsie.

Millie disappeared under the tent flap, and one by one the others slipped in after her.

At that moment Mem decided to let them go without her. She wanted to explore this new world outside the Big Top before she went in to see the performance. Never before had she seen animals or humans behaving like this.

A person dressed in shrill yellow practiced a handspring only a twig's length from where she sat. Nobody took any notice when his head fell off. Mem stared at the orange blot on the ground, till the man scooped it up and lobbed it on again.

"Phew!" she breathed. "It's only hair."

"Out of the way, Cornelius!" The ringmaster waved his decorated cane at the clown. He wore a beaded jacket and jodhpurs, and looked as if he was in charge of the place.

Mem giggled. Wait till she told Magnus and Miranda about this! She wondered if Murgatroyd knew that people took off their hair.

She heard a *yip yip* behind the horses and turned to see a monkey in the arms of a young woman. It leapt to the ground, ran around in a circle, and bounced back into her arms. All the time it yipped and yabbered, but Mem couldn't understand a word.

She scrabbled between the feet of actors and animals, anxious to see what else was part of a circus. Magnus had said it was a dangerous place. But it was exciting, too.

A troupe of acrobats was warming up for the trapeze. They turned backflips and tossed one another through the air as if they were rubber balls. Mem dodged the flying bodies and followed her nose through a fence to a low, dark hill.

"I could get a much better view from the top," she said to herself. "But I don't know what this is." She sniffed around the edges. It smelled warm and earthy.

A kind of bridge stood before her, leading her on. She stepped on to the narrow tip and edged upwards. The ground was spongy under her feet. Up she crept, over the ridges till she came to a smooth section between two small mounds. She stopped to see how far she could climb and found herself gazing into a round, dark eye.

She pulled back and looked around. On the other side, another eye watched her.

"What are you?" asked Mem. "I think you might be alive. Are you some sort of creature?" She glanced back at the bridge that had brought her here. "Is that thing your nose? I've never seen anything like it before."

Would she hang on or make a run for it? While she tried to make up her mind, the gate clicked and she felt the ground move under her.

Murgatroyd had told her stories of how the ground shook, and of rumblings inside the earth. Just like this.

"Hey there, Banjara, time to go!" called the trainer.

In that moment, the world heaved and lurched and the hill grew into a mountain on legs. Mem peered down the slope, and it was too far to fall. She clung to the rough surface but felt her grip slipping as the trainer flung an embroidered saddle over the top.

She scurried for shelter, along a furrow and over a bump till she came to a hollow hidden from view. Inside, it was like a cave. She scratched about and wriggled into a comfortable spot.

"Ahhh!" Mem heard what sounded like a contented sigh. "Ahhh!"

From outside came a girl's voice. "I'm ready, Dad. How's Banjara's ear today?"

The trainer patted Banjara on the trunk. "Right now she doesn't seem as scratchy, wouldn't you say? Nothing worse than a bite from one of those whopper flies. It's a bit hard for a poor old elephant to scratch her ear."

If this is an elephant, thought Mem, then I must be inside its ear. She found herself giggling again. *I'm inside an elephant's ear!* No one would believe her.

"Poor old elephant," the man had said. Mem knew what it was like to have an itchy ear. But if a mosquito bit her, she could twist around and give a good scratch. An elephant wasn't shaped like a mouse, so perhaps a mouse could help. It would be a good thing, to make an elephant happy.

Mem scratched around again and wriggled into a cosy spot. That's what you like, isn't it? A good scratch.

"Ahhh!" she heard.

Keep on scratching, she decided.

The trainer hoisted the girl on to the saddle on the elephant's back.

"And now, Ladies and Gentlemen," shouted the announcer. "We've saved the best till last. Put your hands together for Banjara, the world's most Majestic, most Mercurial, most Magnificent Elephant!"

"Right, then, Banjara, we're on!" said the trainer.

Mem swayed with the elephant as they made their entrance. Music played and people clapped.

"Go on, Banjara," whispered the girl. "Show them you're Boss of the Ring." She tapped her with a cane, and Banjara raised her trunk to salute the audience.

Mem heard the crowd, but could see only the ravines and crannies of the ear and a red lump bigger than a mouse's foot where a fly had bitten the skin.

"I'll just scratch around the edge a bit," she said. "There, is that better?"

"Ahhh!" murmured the elephant. "Ahhh!"

"Glad you like it."

"Keep it up, Banjara," said the girl. "You're doing well this afternoon."

The elephant rocked around the ring and plumped on her backside in the sawdust. Mem held on.

"Up, up," called the trainer.

One after the other, Banjara stretched her hind legs out in front, lifted her forelegs in the air and sat, waiting for the applause.

"Cool!" said the girl. "The best yet."

Banjara held her trunk aloft so the crowd could see the grin on her mouth.

Mem clung to her spot inside the ear as Banjara jolted back to her feet. Circus sounds reverberated all around. A trapeze artist stood on a landing near the roof and pitched a swing into the air. As it came back to him, he caught the bar and swung away with it. In great wheels, he swept across the tent high above the audience heads, now with his hands on the bar, now with his legs looped over it and his arms flying free.

The girl stood on Banjara's back, eyes watching him, lips moving as if she were counting the seconds. The boy swung low over her head and swept her up with him. Hands linked, they reeled above the crowd till the girl suddenly let go.

The audience cried out and some people covered their eyes. The girl somersaulted and landed on her feet on Banjara's back. As the crowd broke into cheers,

the boy dropped from the air and landed on the saddle beside the girl.

Banjara steadied herself and stood firm.

People whistled and cheered. Mem had never heard such a racket. She couldn't imagine what was going on out there. She was stuck in the darkness and she wanted to see. The others would be watching the performance. It might be an idea to show herself. If she climbed out now, she could give them a wave and they'd know she was safe.

Mem crept to the edge of the ear and peeped out. She clawed her way to smoother ground and climbed to the top of Banjara's head, between the two giant flapping ears.

There, Mem stood and gazed about her.

The audience gasped. They clapped their hands and stamped their feet.

"It's a mouse!" said a girl in the front row.

A man near the back grabbed his binoculars, then dropped them back across his knees. "You need a telescope to see that."

Mem gazed down the trunk and cried, "You really are an elephant, aren't you?"

The grin was still there on the elephant's face. "And are you *really* a mouse?" it seemed to be saying.

"I am, I am," Mem cried, and waved a paw to the audience.

The spotlight zoomed down and captured her in its beam. People rose in their seats and shouted and stamped till she thought the roof would blow off the tent.

The boy waved and the girl didn't stop smiling. Smiling and waving.

Mem peered at the layers of seats and saw only a blur of colors mingling together. She couldn't pick out the others in that confusion of confetti faces.

She couldn't possibly hear Manuel gasp under the front row of chairs. "L-l-l-look! It's Mem!"

"What's she doing there?" asked Manfred.

Meggsie bit his bottom lip and glared at him. "Don't ask stupid questions! How do we know what she thinks she's doing?" He shook his paw at Millie. "And don't sing! This is serious."

"What'll we do, then?" wailed Manfred.

Meggsie's jaw drooped. "I wish I knew." Murgatroyd had always warned them, "Beware of big feet," and elephants had the biggest feet of all. "I think we should try and catch her at the exit. Come on now."

They scurried under the row of seats and hid behind a bin near the tent opening.

Mem didn't see them leave. She was concentrating on keeping her balance on the elephant's head while they did one last circuit of the ring.

"Brilliant!" said the ringmaster to the trainer. "Where did you get the mouse?"

He laughed. "It just appeared! Like magic!"

"Then catch it before it disappears. We'll be the only circus in the world with a duo act like this! For years magicians have been pulling rabbits out of a hat, but we pull a mouse out of an elephant's ear!" He shook his head but couldn't shake the grin from his face. "You wouldn't believe it!"

Mem clambered back inside the ear to give herself time to think.

"Ahhh!" breathed the elephant.

"Hey! Where's it gone?" The trainer's voice was desperate.

"Vanished!" said the girl. "Just like it came!" She leaned towards the elephant's head. "I always knew Banjara was special."

The elephant left the ring with a spring in her step, as if she knew something no one else did. Mem gave another scratch to show she was still there.

"Ahhh! Ahhh!"

Meggsie and the others pushed forward as the elephant neared the exit. They grappled with each other to catch a glimpse of Mem.

"Not a trace," said Meggsie.

"Where's she gone?" asked Manfred.

Meggsie sighed. "Will you cut the stupid questions!"

"V-v-v-vanished!" said Manuel and flopped to the ground.

Gone.

# Nine

Magnus darted from bush to bush along the roadside. Passing cars and trucks showered him with dust. Dogs barked behind fences and birds swooped from the trees.

But nothing could stop him now. A power drove him on, past the town, where loud noises came from a great striped tent, and into open country again. His legs moved like machines, and his head was full of brightly colored pictures.

He kept on going as the sun slid into the valley. Somewhere ahead, past the pine plantation, he would come upon the stand of white-trunked gum trees he'd seen in the magazine. Then he'd find the house.

Around a bend, he came to a cluster of buildings surrounded by parked cars. A stale-sweet smell drifted through open doors of the tallest building. Glasses clinked, and in the babble of voices he couldn't hear a word.

*Accommodation* said a sign above the door.

Magnus decided this must be a hotel—surely an important place, with all these people. Perhaps he should stop to check it out. *Hotel* mouse definitely sounded superior to *stable* mouse.

He crept to the doorstep and sniffed about. The smell of beer washed over him and almost knocked him off his feet. The noise hurt his ears. I can do better than this, he thought, and turned back to the road.

The grand house of the magazine could not be far away. Magnus reminded himself he'd set out to find that house and only that. He must keep going.

In the distance the white trunks of the special gums stood like ghosts against the sky. Lights glowed through the trees, beckoning him on.

Before him, the trees inclined their branches to form an arch across the roadway. Sunset wrapped a golden gloss around their limbs and tinged Magnus's coat with gold. The sun's last lingering rays captured the small gleam of his coat and the matching glow on the tall tree trunks, so that anyone happening to pass at that moment might think they were in an enchanted forest.

Magnus was carried away by the greatness of it.

This was the road to the grand house. He was almost there.

He paused, breathless, at the towering gates. Yes, this was it! Exactly as it looked in the picture, except for a sign on the fence.

FOR SALE

MOST DESIRABLE COUNTRY MANSION

INSPECTION BY APPOINTMENT ONLY

It was certainly desirable. In all his time in the city and the country, Magnus hadn't ever seen a more desirable house. Miranda would desire it too, he was sure. For a moment he wished he'd found a minute to tell her where he was going. He could have stopped, too, to check on the young at the circus. He pushed the thoughts from his mind. Just look at this place!

*Country Mansion!* Better even than *hotel.* Anybody could go to a hotel.

He slipped under the gate and walked slowly up the circular drive. Two cars stood on either side of the front entrance. The door was open, and he could hear voices.

The tiles in the entry hall were cold under his feet. He hurried into the first room on the right, where he could see four shiny black shoes and two high heels that glinted when they moved.

"And here we have the library," said a man dressed like a city person.

"Excellent!" said the second man.

"Superb!" said the woman. "Now could we see the kitchen?"

Magnus scampered away before they noticed him. A passage that seemed to go on forever led to a place of more promising smells. Every surface was wiped clean, but the whiff of food hung above the cooking alcove. The man and the woman moved about, flicking switches, turning knobs and taps, and opening cupboards and drawers.

"Stunning!" said the woman. "But a rotisserie is essential."

The almost-city man looked at his watch. "Upstairs, of course, we have five bedrooms . . ."

A bed would be nice, thought Magnus. While the people inspected the kitchen, he ran up the stair rail to the main bedroom. All that space! But not many places for a mouse to hide.

The next two bedrooms were almost as big and not at all designed for a mouse. Magnus moved back to the landing and squeezed under the next door, which turned out to be a cupboard, a linen cupboard. This was more like it!

Memories of his first home with the Musculus family came flooding back—the soft blankets and cosy comfort of the top shelf. There was something about a linen cupboard.

He nodded knowingly and paused to peep under the next door. A second linen cupboard. In a country mansion there was a choice. He could go back to the family and say, "Which would you like, the blankets or the towels?"

And if by chance one turned out to be unsuitable, they could simply move on to the other.

Magnus gazed at the neat stacks of soft, pale bath towels. He longed to curl in the folds and sleep, but the urge to take home the news tugged him away. He turned and scurried back into the street.

# Ten

People were leaving the circus. They jostled between seats and spilled across the grass to the road.

"Watch out," whispered Meggsie, and pushed Millie behind the wheel of a caravan.

There were only four of them now.

"What can we do?" asked Manuel. "I think we should f-follow the elephant."

For the first time, Meggsie couldn't think what to say. They all looked at him and waited. His eyes narrowed into grim slits. "Mem wasn't on the elephant when it left the ring."

"She didn't f-f-fall?" Manuel cringed at the thought of Mem under the elephant's foot.

"Don't think like that!" snapped Meggsie. "If she didn't leave on the elephant, she must still be somewhere in the tent."

He sent them back to search under every seat till they found her.

So while they ferreted under the seats, they didn't see the elephant strolling back to her pen.

In her hiding place Mem heard a rumbling and it was her own stomach. She realized it was almost feed time and there was nothing to eat here. She'd starve to death in an elephant's ear. I'll have to get out, she said to herself. But when? And where will I go?

A mixture of fear and excitement churned inside her chest. Her heart beat faster. She should find the others and tell them she was safe. Yet she didn't want her adventure to stop.

She gave Banjara an extra scratch and poked her nose into the paling light.

"There it is!" shouted the trainer. "Grab it!"

The girl held him back. "Gently, Dad! Wait till it comes down for food. I'll catch it then."

"Just make sure you don't lose it," he said. "It could be worth a lot to us." He clapped a chain around Banjara's front leg and gave her a hefty slap. "Today you get an extra big feed, old girl. For an extra-good performance."

Mem wondered what elephants ate and if there might be anything for her. When the trainer went off to get the meal, she picked her way across the huge shoulders and along the spine toward the tail. It was a long way to the ground. I can't get down that way, she thought. "Beware of big feet," Murgatroyd had said. She hesitated, peering this way and that over the elephant's hide.

Then she heard a whisper. "Come down, little one. Here, come."

The girl was standing on a chair beside Banjara. Her arms reached out to Mem.

Mem narrowed her eyes and pulled back. Did she dare go near a human?

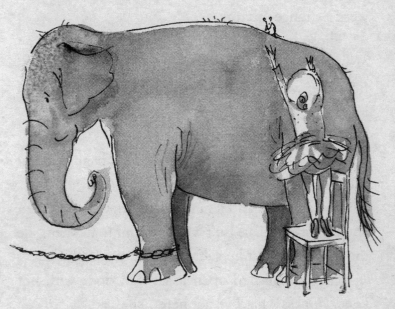

Her foot slipped under her, and she grappled to stay on the elephant's back. She dug her claws into the wrinkly skin and stared at the girl.

The girl smiled at Mem. "Come on, don't be afraid." Her teeth were white and blunt, not like mice teeth at all. Her hair was straw-yellow and thick, and swayed around her neck when she moved. Mem hadn't seen a coat like it before.

Mem stretched out her neck and sniffed. The girl's fingernails smelled like merry-go-round horses and were the khaki color of koala droppings. Humans were a strange mixture.

Those hands could crush me just as easily as an elephant's foot could, thought Mem. Yet the sensations that wafted against her whiskers were warm and inviting.

Mem sidled closer.

"There," said the girl and closed her hands around Mem's body.

It was dark and cramped in there, and Mem couldn't move. This isn't what I meant to happen, she thought as she felt herself carried through the air.

The girl pushed open a caravan door with her knee. "Guess what I've got here," she said.

Her young brother stood up from his computer and stared at her hands. "Tell me."

"Guess."

"I heard about the show. It . . . it isn't . . . ?"

"The mouse!"

"Let me look."

"In a minute." The girl pointed to the back of the van. "Why don't you empty the junk out of that box? We can put it there for now."

She opened her fingers and released Mem into a big supermarket carton.

"It's so small!" cried the boy. "And what happened to its tail?"

"That's funny, I hadn't noticed. It's stumpy!"

The boy bent over the box. "It doesn't matter. It's still quite cute, I reckon. What are we going to do with it?"

The girl raised her eyes to the ceiling. "Dad says we're going to make a fortune."

"Where are we going to keep it?"

"Here, in the van. You can look after it."

The boy smiled. "I'll have to make it a proper house, then."

"First thing is to feed it," said the girl. She fetched

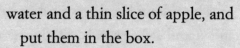

water and a thin slice of apple, and put them in the box.

Mem curled in a corner and twitched her whiskers. The apple smelled juicy-sweet, but she felt a need to be wary.

The boy kneeled beside the box and held out the apple to Mem. "Here, try this." His voice was gentle, coaxing. Mem edged toward him and stretched her neck till her nose almost touched his fingers.

"Come on."

She reached out and nibbled the tip of the apple slice.

"Good?" said the boy.

Mem ate the rest of it.

"She liked it. What else is there?"

"Mice will eat anything, I think, but we'd better find out what's good for them. Cornelius has seed for his parrot. I'll go along and ask him for some."

The boy took out his paints and began to decorate a second, bigger carton; a window here, there an archway and there a door till the box began to look like a castle. "Later, I'll put on a tower," he said.

When the caravan door opened, he jumped up to greet his father. "Hey, Dad, look what we've got!"

"I know all about it," said the trainer. "You make sure you look after it now." He bent down and peered at Mem as if she were the first mouse he'd ever seen. "D'you know, for some reason I think Banjara actually *likes* that mouse. I've never known her so relaxed, especially since the problem with her ear."

The girl returned with some birdseed and sprinkled a few grains into the box.

"Give it a good feed," said her father. "It's on again tonight."

"So you really mean it?" said the girl. "A performing mouse!"

"Sure I do. I wouldn't keep a thing like that around the place just for the fun of it."

The boy bent over Mem and whispered, "Never mind. I'll look after you." He shredded some paper and spread it in the box. "This'll keep you warm."

Mem sat back and twitched her nose at him. She hadn't studied a human so closely before. He didn't look bad at all, and he was kind. He could even become a friend. Yet she wasn't sure she liked being in a box. There was so much in the world outside, and she couldn't see any of it. She couldn't see a way out, either.

For now she didn't feel in danger. She nibbled the seeds and thought it was the easiest meal she'd ever found.

Mem hunched in a corner of the box and shut her eyes. It was not yet dark outside, and she'd been awake all day. The man said something was going to happen tonight, and she had a feeling she'd need all her energy.

She listened to the slurp and clatter of the family dinner. As soon as they'd finished eating, the trainer and his daughter changed back into circus dress and waved good night to the boy. They picked up the box with Mem in it and carried it off for the evening performance.

"I'll have the new box finished when you get back," called the boy.

When the trainer placed Mem on the elephant's back, Banjara flicked her trunk as if to say hello. Mem peered over the bristly head to look for a moment into her eye. She was sure Banjara saw her there.

"Quork!" She heard the squawk at the same time

as the flap of wings above her. She dove to the shelter of the ear and sat there shivering.

"Help!" yelled the girl.

"Cornelius! Get your parrot off!" shouted the trainer.

"Sorry, mate," said the clown. "You didn't tell me about the mouse."

"What *else* is there in a circus?" wondered Mem, as she huddled in the darkness. She'd better be more careful.

She gazed around her hiding spot and saw the lump from the insect bite. She gave a little scratch around the edges.

"Ahhh! Ahhh!"

"It's not so big now," said Mem. "It's getting better. And now I'm here, I can keep the flies away."

"Ahhh! Ahhh!"

"Attention, Ladies and Gentlemen! We've saved the best till last. Put your hands together for Everybody's Favorite Elephant, the World's most Majestic, most Mercurial, most Magnificent Banjara!"

"Hold on," Mem told herself. "Here we go!" She sat there and listened to the trainer's instructions and the girl's talk as the elephant went through her paces.

Mem clung to the ear when Banjara sat in the sawdust, and waited for the thud of the acrobats landing on her rump.

The act went without a hitch. And Mem waited for her moment. "My turn!" she squeaked, and emerged from the ear.

The spotlight shone on her, alone on the elephant's head.

"Here I am!" she squealed, and waved both front paws to the crowd.

The applause was tumultuous. Mem beamed at the people and bowed to every side of the tent. She couldn't see Meggsie and the others, but supposed they'd be safely home by now.

She hoped they'd enjoyed the afternoon performance.

# Eleven

Darkness screened the road ahead, but Magnus knew the way. Headlights captured him in their beam, blinding him for a second before they swept past.

Magnus felt satisfied with himself. In the cool of the night, he ran faster. He'd be back before morning. Soon, soon he'd be telling them!

"Now listen," he'd say. And he'd pause to make sure they were all quiet. "I've found something super special. You won't believe it till you see it. We'll be the smartest mice in this whole world."

He could just see the surprise on their faces!

As dawn filtered through the darkness, he climbed the ladder to the loft.

"Here I am!"

The mice stood, eyes down, and nobody spoke.

"Don't you want to know where I've been?" He looked at them, standing silently in front of him. "Is anything wrong?" His voice grew more urgent. "What's happened?"

Miranda stepped towards him. "Mem's missing!"

Not Mem! "Missing? You mean, lost?"

Miranda caught her breath and nodded.

"Where? How?" He grabbed her in his paws and shook her.

"Meggsie will tell you."

Meggsie's top teeth drooped over his bottom lip. He shook his head, as if he couldn't bring himself to speak.

"Well, tell me," said Magnus.

"I . . . er . . . at the circus, we went into the tent and Mem didn't follow. When I went out to look, she was gone. We looked and looked, but there was no sign of her. She just disappeared. And then . . . and then . . ."

"Go on!"

"We saw her. In the ring, on the elephant."

"On the *what*?"

"The elephant."

Magnus's face turned pink. "Don't tell me such rubbish."

"It's a f-f-f-fact," said Manuel.

"Yes," said Miranda. "It's true."

"And you left her there?" said Magnus.

"We . . . we've only just come home. We stayed and we looked everywhere, but it was no use."

"Truly, we tr-tried," said Manuel. "Oh, we might n-never see her again!"

Manfred and Millie clung to Miranda and buried their faces in her coat. Their sobs trickled into the silence.

Magnus slumped in the hay. His shoulders began to shake as the young ones' whimpering told him it was true. His Mem was lost. He forgot the country mansion. What did it matter? Nothing else mattered now. Mem had gone.

Why did I let her go to the circus? he thought. If only I'd stayed with them.

"Don't just sit there," said Miranda. "We'll have to do something."

"If only . . . ," murmured Magnus.

"There's no time for '*if only*'s. We have to find her."

Magnus shook himself. "Yes, you're right." He straightened his back till he stood tall among the others. "Now, here's what we'll do."

Magnus called on all the strength that Mortimer and Murgatroyd had given him. The circus was a raucous place, where people and animals lived and worked and attracted other humans from everywhere.

He stood back and counted the caravans. "Some person has taken Mem," he said. "She must be a prisoner. So first thing is to search the caravans. Each mouse takes two caravans, and we'll cover them more quickly."

He pointed to a group of vans under the trees. "Right then, Meggsie, you take the first two over there, Manuel the next two, and so on. Understand? Get going!"

Daylight made their task more dangerous. The midday sun burned down on them as they spread out to the caravans. When Magnus turned to go, Miranda touched him lightly with her paw. "We'll find her. I know we will."

"Yes," said Magnus, though his heart was heavy with doubts.

Under cover of long grass, he ran to the van at the far end of the reserve. He climbed up the wheel and on to a window ledge, and peeped inside.

"Quork!"

Magnus reeled back and almost lost his grip on the ledge.

A white parrot perched on the back of a chair. It fluffed out its feathers and cocked its crest at him. "Quork!"

Magnus breathed out slowly. Apart from the bird, the van appeared deserted. Strange costumes hung from a railing; such clothes he'd never seen on the farm or even in the city. They billowed from hangers in bright yellows and oranges, with spots and stars and crosses.

Beside the sink stood an open packet. Through the window he could smell the seed. If only he had a moment to sneak in there . . . but he couldn't waste time on himself. He sniffed again and detected no trace of Mem in that caravan.

Voices came from the next van. "Can I watch the show this afternoon, seeing it's Saturday? And it is *my* pet!" said a boy.

"I'll fix you up with a seat," said a man. "But get a move on there. We need to check on Banjara first."

The boy stepped from the van, cradling a small box. A man and a girl followed and locked the door behind them.

Magnus nosed up the step and squeezed under the door. A strong human smell gushed over him. But there was more. Magnus would recognize it anywhere. Mem had been here; he was certain of that.

He searched about the small space, and his eyes

were drawn to the toy house on the table. Windows had been painted on the side, with the outline of arches and a door that didn't open. A toilet-roll tower lurched from the roof. It looked like a castle, or even a country mansion, but it was a box.

As he gazed at it his golden dream of the country mansion fell away in a shower of glitter.

He remembered a castle that had once been his cage. A tingle of fear ran through his chest. This, too, could be a prison for a mouse.

He sniffed around the cardboard sides and knew he was right. Mem had been held here, inside that box. Then where was she now?

Magnus wished he'd followed the three humans when they left the van. He was sure now that the boy had been carrying Mem in the small box. They'd taken her away. He had to find them, and quickly.

Magnus darted down the steps with his nose to the ground. He'd lost the scent of Mem, but the heavy human tread was easy to follow. Whiskers pricked, he forged ahead, ignoring the boots and shoes that trampled past on their way to the performance.

He pressed on until the trail stopped and scents mingled together around a fenced area. Magnus raised his snout and sniffed the air. An all-powerful odor drowned out any hint of Mem. In front of him a huge shape swayed against the sky.

This must be the elephant! Magnus slipped through the fence and crouched in the gutter just inside the pen. He watched the enormous animal plod up and down on legs as thick as gum trees. Magnus couldn't tell whether it was coming or going. Horses and cats and dogs have crooked back legs like mice, he thought, but here the front and back legs look exactly alike. This animal had four knees!

"I suppose if that long thing is your nose, then you're coming this way," he said. "But I'm not hanging around any longer." The human trail appeared to lead toward the tent, so he must keep going.

As he turned away, the elephant swished her trunk across the ground and almost swiped Magnus off his feet. He gazed up in shock. When the elephant lifted her trunk, Magnus found himself staring into a gaping nostril. In a flash, he was sucked into a kind of hosepipe and hoisted high in the air.

Before Magnus knew it, the elephant had swung her trunk across her shoulder and blown Magnus into her ear.

"Phew!" Magnus shuddered and patted himself to make sure he was still alive. Where am I? he wondered. It's like night in here. He scratched with his claws to grip the uneven surface.

"Ahhh!" murmured the elephant. "Ahhh!"

I can't stay here, thought Magnus. I'm no use to anyone locked in this place. Yet he couldn't risk being thrown to the ground or being trampled on by those enormous feet. Poor Mem. He'd come to rescue her and he'd let her down. Miranda and the others would be looking for him. "Just give me time to think," he said, "and I'll get out of here."

Sounds from outside drifted to Magnus as if through a muffler. Human voices came closer, but he couldn't see the man and the girl from the caravan, or the boy who lifted Mem from the box and placed her on the elephant's back.

"There you go," said the boy. "I'll be back after the show."

Mem scurried to the fringe of the ear and stretched down so Banjara could see her there. "It's me again!"

The elephant looped her trunk under and up and gave a juicy snort.

"I hope that bite's better now."

Magnus jerked upright and hit his head on a sinewy bulge. He knew that voice!

Mem gripped the flap of the ear and nosed her way to the entrance.

"Magnus! What are you doing here?"

Magnus didn't know whether to scold her or to hug her. "I could ask the same of you!"

He looked her up and down and decided she was unharmed. "Where are we then?"

"This is the elephant's ear. And how did *you* get here?"

"She picked me up and put me here. It's the last place I wanted to be—except that I found you."

Mem twitched her pink nose and nodded. "I suppose she thought you were me. I scratch her ear, see? And she likes me."

The trainer led Banjara towards the Big Top with

the girl in the saddle. She waved to her brother when they entered the ring. Magnus and Mem dug in their claws as they rolled from side to side inside the ear.

"How do we get out of here?" Magnus asked Mem. "I think you know more about this than I do."

"Stay with me, and I'll tell you when to come out."

"Good." Magnus nodded. "As long as it's safe."

"And now, Ladies and Gentlemen, the act you've all been waiting for, the world's most Majestic, most Mercurial, most Magnificent Elephant, Banjara!"

Magnus gritted his teeth and clung on, wondering what would happen next.

The ringmaster held up his arms and flourished his cane. Music swelled. Magnus and Mem lurched back and forth as Banjara sat in the sawdust, then heaved herself back on her feet.

"There'll be other things happening now," said Mem. "Just listen."

The trapeze artist zipped through the air near the top of the tent. He swept the girl from the elephant's back and whirled with her across the heads of the crowd.

The two mice heard the audience screech and then break into cheers and clapping.

"Get ready," said Mem. "It's nearly our turn."

"Our turn . . . ?"

"Go on!" She tapped Magnus on the backside and shoved him into the light.

The audience roared when they appeared on the elephant's head. Mem saw the boy in the front row. His mouth hung open. "Two!" he cried. "It's magic!"

When Mem waved, his face broke into the biggest smile she'd ever seen.

The clapping and cheering and stamping drowned out the music and all other sounds of the town.

The ringmaster's eyes grew as round as golf balls, and nearly as white. The color drained from his face and he fell backwards, mumbling. "Double! Maybe I shouldn't have had that extra beer at lunch."

Mem raised her front paws in the air and thought the applause would never stop. "Wave!" she squeaked to Magnus, and laughed at his wobbly salute. "Hey! Hey!" She leaped on his shoulders and waved both paws.

The trainer stood and stared and wondered whether he was needed as a trainer at all.

"What d'you reckon, Dad!" called the girl. Her beaming smile lit up the air about her. She didn't worry that the ringmaster lay in the sawdust. She didn't know how one mouse had suddenly become two, but there was something magic about the mouse with the stumpy tail.

With the mice up front, she rode Banjara on two extra circuits of the ring before they left the tent.

"What happens to us now?" Magnus asked Mem when the cheering had faded behind them.

"Come back into the ear for a while. They'll be here to get us soon."

Mem settled into a comfortable spot and smiled at Magnus. It was good to see him again.

"I've been thinking," she said. "It might be better tonight if you go into the other ear. Then we could come out from each side and meet in the middle."

Magnus frowned. "What do you mean, tonight? I'm here to take you home."

"Oh!"

"Don't you know, we've been looking for you? We've all been worried."

"Oh!"

"You haven't once asked about the others."

"But I think of them all the time. It's just that I've made friends here."

"They're not like us at all."

She giggled. "Funny, isn't it? I wanted to find friends like me . . ."

"And they couldn't be more different."

Mem's ruby eyes opened wider, as if she still couldn't believe it. "I don't need them to be like me. I know that now."

# Twelve

"Nothing!" said Meggsie.

"Yes, nothing," said Miranda. "Did you find anything, Manuel?"

"N-n-n-nothing."

The mice gathered under a scrubby bush to check one another's search of the caravans. They all shook their snouts. "Not a sign."

"What about Magnus?" asked Millie. "Where's he gone?"

"He'll be back," said Meggsie. "He's probably on to something."

They snuggled into the dirt and listened to waves of laughter and clapping coming from inside the tent. Everything was happening somewhere else. Here, nothing moved. The afternoon air hung like a dead weight and the heat sucked at their spirits.

"Something's gone wrong," said Manfred.

"Don't think like that," said Miranda. "Just

remember what Murgatroyd always said: 'No news is good news.' Perhaps he's found Mem."

But as the sun moved behind the tent and cheers from inside made them feel more like outsiders and still Magnus didn't come, their hopes drained away.

"Not Magnus too!" mumbled Meggsie. He bit his lip so hard that it began to bleed. "What is there about a circus, that we lose each other like this?"

"It's the d-d-disappearing act," said Manuel.

"That's not funny!" snapped Meggsie, though he knew Manuel was serious. First Mem, and now Magnus had vanished. Whatever happened to Mem could have happened to Magnus too.

The crowd was beginning to leave the circus. People poured out of the tent and spread in all directions to their cars.

"What are we going to do without them?" wailed Manfred.

"We'll keep looking," said Meggsie. "But wait till the crowd has gone."

Miranda wagged her whiskers at him. "No, it's time to do something now. We must be strong, and if we can find Magnus, he'll lead us to Mem." Her eyes puckered as she worked out a plan. "We need to think like Magnus and ask ourselves where he might have gone that was different from where each of us went."

None of the mice could get inside Magnus's mind to work out where he might have gone. They stared at the ground with blank faces, and no ideas came to them.

"I think . . . ," said Miranda. "If he found some clue in a van, he'd delve around and follow a trail. Where might it have led him?"

"To where Mem was before she was where she isn't," said Manfred.

"Of course," said Miranda. "Now, listen!" She pointed with her paw. "Those were the two vans Magnus went to search. We'll start there and see what we find."

The first caravan told them nothing, but Miranda knew as soon as she saw the second that it held a clue. She pushed her whiskers and then her head under the door.

"What can you see?" asked Meggsie.

"It's a sort of house."

"I mean, *inside*!"

"It *is* inside; a house in a caravan! I'll have a sniff around. There's nobody here."

The others squeezed under the door after her. "It's

more like a castle," said Meggsie. "And Mem's been in there." He butted the cardboard wall with his head. "But she's not there now."

"It's a p-p-prison," said Manuel.

Miranda screwed up her nose. "I'm sure now Mem's been a prisoner here. Magnus has found that out too. We'll follow his track and see where it leads us. Come on, no giving up!"

They nosed through the grass, keeping close to the ground, and the whiff of Magnus led them on. His trail mingled with the scent of foreign animals and the footsteps of a thousand shoes.

"Keep your heads down," said Miranda. "We're still on the right track."

Then she stopped. They'd been so intent on sniffing the ground that they hadn't looked where they were going. A fence stood in front of them, with the earth scuffed around it. Magnus's trail had ended. Miranda breathed hard, but the scent went nowhere. It was as if he'd vanished into the air.

Inside the elephant's ear Magnus and Mem were in a different world.

"We'll have to get out of here," Magnus said as the elephant swayed around the pen.

"Would you like to have a look from the top?" said Mem.

"But we've come to take you home! We're all here . . ."

"Why?"

Magnus stared at her. "Don't you want to come?"

"Of course, but . . ."

"But what?"

"I'm having a good time here. And there's another show tonight."

Magnus squinted at Mem, trying to peer into her thoughts. "I've seen where they've kept you, and you're not going back to a place like that. And neither am I." Right now, he and Mem were prisoners, yet she didn't seem to realize it. He had to get them away from here. But if he was to escape he needed Mem's guidance.

He watched as she scruffed around and scratched her claws into the rough skin.

"Ahhh!" murmured the elephant. "Ahhh!"

Magnus listened to the deep murmurings and wondered how all this could have come about. Here he was, with Mem, inside a sighing mountain. It was more dangerous than any hill he'd ever climbed, for this moving mountain could trample them to death.

Outside the air hummed with the sounds of humans.

"Call them out now!" said a man whose voice Magnus had heard before.

"Hey, dinner time!" called the boy.

Mem jumped up and scurried to the edge of the cranny. "Did you hear that? It's time to go."

Magnus pounced and held her by the tail. "They'll catch you! You're not going back!"

She wriggled from his grasp and peeped from their hiding place. Only her head was visible, but it was enough. Five small mice looked up at her.

"It's Mem!" squeaked a voice she knew well.

Magnus dragged Mem back into the hole.

"I saw the others!" she told him. "Hiding in the grass, all of them!"

"I hope they'll keep out of the way," he said. "I don't want them to get trampled."

"They're hiding on one side of the elephant, and the people are on the other," said Mem. "And *we're* in the middle."

"Get those mice out!" shouted the trainer.

"How can we get them out?" squealed Meggsie from the other side.

"There's a real commotion out there," said Magnus. "All because of us. I don't think we can leave this place now. The people will catch us. It's a trap."

"Come on, little ones," called the boy.

"That's the one who looks after me," said Mem. "He's kind and he'll feed us. Let's go!"

Magnus gripped the stump of her tail in his teeth. "No way!"

Then he heard Miranda's voice. "Are you there, Magnus? Mem?"

Magnus's jaw dropped at the sound of her voice. He gazed at Mem with a question in his eyes. How could he sit there and not answer Miranda's call? Yet he knew she had the brains to understand the danger.

He tried to put a calm into his voice, though his mind was churning. "Mem, Miranda knows we can't go down now. She'll wait. Humans might not know when mice are around, but Miranda can see and hear those people, every word."

"The boy looked after me, you know," said Mem.

Magnus sighed. "He likes you. And I can tell the elephant likes you too. You've made friends here, but it isn't your home. The circus will move on. Where will it go next? You'll never have a proper home, like ours."

"The elephant would miss me."

"But the circus will come back one day, and you can visit. An elephant never forgets."

"How do you know?"

"I think Murgatroyd told me."

Mem sat back and fluffed herself into a soft ball. For a moment, she was silent. Then she said, "I suppose Murgatroyd will be waiting."

Magnus wiggled his nose and wished he didn't have to tell her now.

"Something's wrong," said Mem. "I can tell by the way you weriggle your nose."

Magnus smiled at her way of talking, and gently drew her to him. "I haven't told you yet, but while you were gone, Murgatroyd died."

Mem drooped her head on her chest. "I knew . . . I felt something wasn't right."

"But it isn't wrong, Mem. He went off knowing he was ready." Magnus rubbed his nose against hers. "At the end, he was the real Murgatroyd. He told me to keep out of his way!"

Mem sighed. "So much has happened, and now I can't tell him. But I'm not sorry for Murgatroyd, because I know he's gone into always."

In their cramped shelter, Magnus smiled at her. "Good! Then how would Murgatroyd have solved our problem here?"

"He would ask what is important to me. And I want to stay for one more show."

His jaw stiffened. "You're not serious!"

"Just one more performance! You can watch, if you'd rather. Miranda hasn't seen the show, either."

Magnus gave up. "If that's really what you want— and then you'll come home?"

"I promise."

The voices from outside were fewer now and quieter. "I'm hungry," said the boy. "Can I leave some food for my mouse and come back later?"

"Yes, it's nearly dark," said his father. "I've got better things to do than hang around waiting for some mice."

The boy looked over his shoulder as they walked away. "They'll be all right, won't they?"

The man grunted, and the voices faded with their footsteps.

"Let's see what's down there now," said Mem.

She and Magnus edged from the ear and climbed to the elephant's head. "Are you there, Miranda?" called Magnus.

The ground erupted and five noses spurted above the grass. Five mice squealed and cheered and waved their paws. "It's them!" shouted Meggsie. "Both of them!"

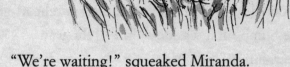

"We're waiting!" squeaked Miranda.

"I knew you would be." Magnus smiled down at her. "We won't be long!"

"Banjara will have a sleep soon," Mem told Magnus. "And then we'll leave the way I first came."

"The front or the back way?" asked Magnus.

Mem pointed to the trunk, which dangled drowsily. "Down there."

The elephant began to sway. Mem dug her claws into the wrinkled shoulder. "She's getting sleepy. You'd better hang on."

Banjara heaved one way and then the other, plunged to her knees, and dropped like a ton of cushions on to her side.

"We're there," whispered Mem. "She's down."

"Then let's go." Magnus stood behind Mem and told her to lead the way. She nosed across the forehead and down the slope between the eyes to the start of the bridge.

"Come on, now."

Magnus twitched his nose in answer. He was concentrating on not slipping down the precipice. He followed Mem across the domed forehead and over the hump till it was downhill all the way.

"Now, jump!" said Mem.

The two mice stood for a second on the tip of the trunk, then dived to the grass. They picked themselves up and bounded away.

The others rushed towards them. They laughed and sang and hugged one another and couldn't stop patting Mem.

Millie rubbed noses with Mem and stood back to look at her. "Is it really you?"

"Of course I'm me." Mem wiggled her whiskers at Millie. "Who else could I be?"

"She's a f-f-f-fact!" said Manuel, and they all jumped on him and cuffed him with their paws.

Manfred and Millie linked paws with Mem, and the three of them sat like a jigsaw that had finally fitted together.

"We're hungry," said Mem. "What about the rest of you?" She sniffed her way to the bowl of grain the boy had left them. "And there's carrot, too. Who wants some?"

They all scrambled for their share of the meal.

"It's a f-f-feast," said Manuel with carrot on his snout.

"And afterward," said Mem, "afterward, I want you to come and see the show."

They looked at one another, questioning.

"My last show," she said.

"All right," said Miranda. "I think I'd like to see it."

Mem reached out and touched Miranda with her paw. "And then we'll go home."

# Thirteen

"Ladies and Gentlemen, once again we are proud to introduce the world's most celebrated Elephant, the most Majestic, most Mercurial, most Magnificent—and indeed the most Magical—Banjara!"

Banjara strode into the ring with the girl on her back, and on her head stood a small white mouse.

The spotlight captured Mem in its beam, and never left her.

She balanced there, spinning in circles and waving to the audience.

"She's a star!" whispered Miranda.

"Yes," said Magnus.

The mice tapped their feet to join the cheering, stamping crowd.

Mem stood still, like a white china mouse, while the trapeze artists flew above her head. She bowed to them and clapped when they landed on Banjara's back. They stood in their glittering bodystockings,

flung out their arms, and blew kisses to the smallest
star of the show.

The elephant raised her trunk in salute. The finger
on the end beckoned to Mem. She hopped into its
clasp and felt herself lifted high in the air. Banjara
paraded around the ring, cradling Mem in the loop of
her trunk, holding her for all the audience to see.

The crowd clapped and cheered and whistled long after the elephant and the tiny mouse had left the ring.

When they reached the yard, Mem crawled back into Banjara's ear and whispered, "Thank you for having me."

Her trumpet of farewell could be heard as far away as the farm, where almost everybody was asleep.

In the cover of evening, the seven mice started their journey home. Mem scuttled up to Magnus and tugged at his shoulder. "Do you think we could go past the caravan . . . the one where I lived? I'll show the others."

As they neared the van, she asked them all to stop. "This is the place. Come and see."

Miranda shivered as Mem climbed up the ledge to the window. "We've all seen the house, Mem. Now let's keep going."

Mem stood and peeped into the caravan. There was the box painted to look like a castle, empty on the floor. The man and the girl and the boy were sitting at the table, eating big bowls of pasta and peas. Mem liked peas. The boy's black hair flopped over his face as he ate. Then, for an instant, he looked up. Mem was sure he saw her there at the window. She pressed her nose against the glass, but he bent his head back over his bowl.

"You'll need to round up those mice soon," said the man.

"They'll be right," said the boy, but for a moment his eyes clouded when he gazed at the empty castle.

"Good-bye," whispered Mem, and hurried off to join the others.

# Fourteen

**W**ithin sight of the farm, the mice stopped to rest. High above, the moon pushed through the clouds, throwing a silver light on the stable roof.

A warm contentment washed through Magnus, now he was back with his family. He gazed at Mem, at her white coat shining on the grass, and the moment became special because she was there. "I'm glad you're back," he said.

From the corner of his eye, he saw a new-moon grin beside a prickle bush. He turned his head. "You're here!"

The kitten beamed at him.

Magnus crept closer and twitched his whiskers at the kitten. "Have you come to welcome us back?"

The kitten smacked her tongue around her mouth.

"I know you're my friend."

The kitten swished her paw and slapped him out of the way.

Magnus stumbled to his feet and stared at her. "I'm not sure I trust you after all."

Mem rested her paw on Magnus's neck. "Leave it to me. I'm a friend." She turned to the kitten as if she were part of the family. "Are you coming with us to the stable?"

The kitten stretched and began to purr.

"Does she have to?" asked Miranda.

"Shh!" said Magnus. "Wait and see."

The kitten bent down and licked Mem's nose with her sandpaper tongue. Mem steadied herself and wiped her nose with her paw.

"She almost knocked you off your f-f-feet," said Manuel.

"It's her way," said Mem. "I'm all right."

The kitten yawned, blew out a steamy blast of breath, then turned and slinked toward the house.

"Good!" said Meggsie. "I feel better without her around."

"Don't be horrible!" said Mem. "Why couldn't she stay?"

Miranda saw the disappointment in Mem's eyes and moved beside her. "You and the kitten can still get along, but she has her own place, just like we do."

"Yes," said Magnus. He sidled closer to Miranda, who was nearly as wise as Murgatroyd.

She prodded him with her nose. "I've been meaning to ask you something. Where were you all that time, when Mem first went missing?"

Magnus felt the warmth of her soft coat against his. He gazed toward the silvered roof, where their snuggery lay waiting.

"I was looking . . . I was finding out that there's nowhere as good as our stable."

"Of course," she said. "We're here for always."

In the stable the horses were stirring. The roan lifted his head and whinnied to the waking world. It was time for the mice to return home, to sleep away the day.

"Yes," said Magnus again. Always had the right smell about it.

# Have you read all of the books in the Harvey Angell trilogy?

Harvey Angell brightens up orphan Henry's life like a supercharged thunderbolt, and nothing will ever be the same again! But Harvey Angell's true identity is a mystery—one that Henry's got to solve!

While on a seaside vacation Henry discovers the ghost of an unhappy girl haunting his rental house. None of the lodgers is going to get any sleep until Henry and Harvey uncover the shocking secrets of Sibbald House.

Henry finds an extraordinary baby hidden in his garden—a baby with tiny antennae instead of eyebrows, and ears that look like buttercups! Henry's running out of time, and he has to find Harvey Angell before this mystery turns into a cosmic disaster.

Aladdin Paperbacks • Simon & Schuster Children's Publishing Division
www.SimonSaysKids.com

# Test your detective skills with these spine-tingling Aladdin Mysteries!

The Star-Spangled Secret
By K. M. Kimball

Mystery at Kittiwake Bay
By Joyce Stengel

Scared Stiff
By Willo Davis Roberts

O'Dwyer & Grady
Starring in Acting Innocent
By Eileen Heyes

Ghosts in the Gallery
By Barbara Brooks Wallace

## The York Trilogy By Phyllis Reynolds Naylor

Shadows on the Wall

Faces in the Water

Footprints at the Window

# ALADDIN CLASSICS

## ALL THE BEST BOOKS FOR CHILDREN
## AND THEIR FAMILIES TO READ!

*THE SECRET GARDEN*
by Frances Hodgson Burnett
Foreword by E. L. Konigsburg
0-689-83141-2

*TREASURE ISLAND*
by Robert Louis Stevenson
Foreword by Avi
0-689-83212-5

*ALICE'S ADVENTURES IN*
*WONDERLAND*
by Lewis Carroll
Foreword by Nancy Willard
0-689-83375-X

*LITTLE WOMEN*
by Louisa May Alcott
Foreword by Joan W. Blos
0-689-83531-0

*THE HOUND OF THE BASKERVILLES*
by Sir Arthur Conan Doyle
Foreword by Bruce Brooks
0-689-83571-X

*THE WIND IN THE WILLOWS*
by Kenneth Grahame
Foreword by Susan Cooper
0-689-83140-4

*THE WIZARD OF OZ*
by L. Frank Baum
Foreword by Eloise McGraw
0-689-83142-0

*THE ADVENTURES OF*
*HUCKLEBERRY FINN*
by Mark Twain
Foreword by Gary Paulsen
0-689-83139-0

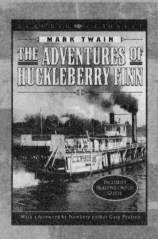